ENTER VENUS

A Fairy Tale
for Adults

Sondra Luger

authorHOUSE®

AuthorHouse™
1663 Liberty Drive
Bloomington, IN 47403
www.authorhouse.com
Phone: 1 (800) 839-8640

Published by AuthorHouse   08/27/2016

ISBN: 978-1-5246-2554-2 (sc)
ISBN: 978-1-5246-2552-8 (hc)
ISBN: 978-1-5246-2553-5 (e)

Library of Congress Control Number: 2016913730

Print information available on the last page.

Previously Published Books by Sondra Luger:

RICH, NEVER MARRIED, RICH
BACK FROM BORA BORA
DROP ME OFF IN HARLEM
MURDER ON BROADWAY

Chapter One

JANE SURVEYED THE DISARRAY. THE room looked frail and desolate, as though suffering from chronic pinkeye, despite the opulent clutter and her presence in its midst. There was surely a rational approach to discovering its whereabouts — the brooch that is, the beautiful ruby-studded brooch Alan had bought her for their first anniversary. She stumbled over a pile of lamé and brocade heaped at the foot of the bed and regained her balance at the open door of the closet, awash with the pastels she loved only a shade less than herself. She grimaced and rubbed the spot where she imagined some sequins had brushed her leg, oblivious of the fact that the sequined dresses still hung on their padded hangers in the closet. The brooch had been a favorite since its receipt, and although she hadn't worn it often she had always savored the pleasure of its possession during those nooks and crannies of time when despondency overtook her. Like the time she had been asked to straighten out the muddle of arrangements for the flower show, and the time St. Barnaby's Home for the Indigent and Aged had begged her to solicit bequests from the nouveau riche youngsters who now crowded a once sedate ballroom a mere block away. And somehow she had gotten through. Beautifully, in fact. She had been hailed as nonpareil at orchestrating flowers and their human tangents and superb at solicitation. The brooch was her talisman. She was vague about why she felt she needed it just now. She felt no pangs of inadequacy or depression. Quite the contrary. She was elated. Her thirty-sixth birthday was a source of celebration and satisfaction to her. She was still able to catch the eye as well as the ear of men and felt wonderful and young. Her only uneasiness centered on the brooch. Still, she had time before the flowers, the fuss and the opera. Yes, she had discovered Alan's secret this year as always. A brief wonder at her disinclination to be surprised flitted across her mind. She threw herself across the bed, pulled open the top drawer of her night table, and removed the pink book that itemized her social obligations and pleasures of the year to date. She noted that she had last worn the brooch three months earlier at the anniversary party friends had given her and Alan to celebrate their sixth year together. It had graced her white woolen dress as a pendant. And indeed, it was with her collection of hanging jewels, still on the silver chain. She held it up to the light. The silver giraffe, his mouth set in an endearing, full, and foolish smile, winked at her all his ruby-spotted length. She removed him from the chain and placed him carefully among friends in an extensive jeweled clip-on ménage. She penciled a notation in the pink book. Now she would remember.

★★★★★

"But Mrs. Blaiser, you don't understand. The public is crying out for representational art. They don't want to be shown a Rorschach blot and be told that it's a cat, or a mash of brown and green squiggles and be told that it's a tree. They want to see things as they really are. Those framed gobs of paint out there don't speak to the average person. And let's face it — most of us are average."

"Mr. Leroy, you have most winning manners. You attack my understanding, my stature and the artists this gallery represents, and you expect to succeed in persuading me to accept your work."

"No, I don't."

"Oh, well then, you have succeeded admirably. Why did you come here, anyway? Surely you know we deal solely in abstract art."

"I thought you might appreciate a crack at something new. At least something so old that it's more novel than new. And I saw your picture in one of the trade magazines and figured that a beautiful woman might be interested in hanging some beautiful art, don't you see?"

Jane fingered the giraffe brooch and suppressed a smile. "You see and I perceive. Your paintings are pretty, and I'm sure you'll find a proper outlet for them."

The young man shook his head. "I don't think so. I've tried just about everywhere. But you do think they're pretty?"

"Yes. Good day, Mr. Leroy." She pressed a button on the desk. "Angie, tell Phil to bring in the ad copy for the spread in *Gourmet.*"

She thumbed through the appointment calendar on her desk. It was nine o'clock. At ten a meeting with Jordan James about a possible fall show, at ten-thirty ditto with Gordon Hassler, at noon lunch with Maggie French and a reporter from *Flower Children Magazine* to discuss personality and character of flowers as depicted in Maggie's paintings. Jane had insisted on being present, because no, Maggie could not speak for herself, at least not without getting into a lawsuit. One near-miss was enough for Jane Blaiser's favorite client. At three o'clock she would examine what George had come up with in the way of a new contract for Carson Trumbull and check on preparations for his upcoming show. She ruefully recalled her last meeting with him. Mr. Leroy has a point, she thought. Artists like Trumbull do want to "see things as they really are" — profusely green and bankable. Economic not artistic reality. But being of a realistic business bent herself, she knew that the popular Trumbull, churning out work as he did, was producing a glutted market, and before long no market at all for his work. She toyed with the idea of not renewing his contract. She would get short-term notoriety for insanity and long-term kudos for foresight. The publicity a Trumbull-Blasier brouhaha would generate would be both free and lucrative. She frowned. George had been working hard on the contract. But her eyes danced: BLAISER DROPS TRUMBULL! The show would be exciting, especially

3

exciting. The end would be like the beginning, only a doubly big deal. There was a knock on the door.

"Come in, Phil." She closed her appointment book with satisfaction, then fingered the button again. "Angie, no calls 'til eleven o'clock."

★★★★★

Alan Blaiser pulled his coat collar closer to his face. Jane had warned him it was spring in name only and that he had better not discard his woolen coat just yet, but he hadn't listened to her. Some red and yellow tulips along Park Avenue bobbed in the breeze. He clenched his teeth. The weather would just have to learn to cooperate with the calendar. His shoulders hunched forward, he turned down 64th Street and walked toward Lexington Avenue. Jane would be surprised. He enjoyed catching her at off moments and treasured those few occasions when he had succeeded. He had canceled all morning appointments. Digby would rearrange them for him, taking some himself. At the corner of Lexington Avenue he made two purchases, a newspaper and a cornucopia of flowers. He discarded all but several sheets of the newspaper, wrapping the remainder around the flowers.

"Spring is news!" he beamed at the vendor. He continued down Lexington for half a block, eyes bright, nose red.

★★★★★

"I'll announce you, Mr. Blaiser," she said doubtfully, "but it will throw Jane off if you just march in. That *Gourmet* spread is turning out to be ticklish work, and there is a deadline."

"That's all right, Angie," he said bravely. "I can wait." He bent over her appointment book. "She can squeeze me in before Mr. — uh — Jordan."

"That's Mr. James."

"Yes, well, whatever. But perhaps my flowers can get in earlier?"

"I'm really sorry, but it will —"

"Only throw her off, I know."

"I'll put them in water." She reached out for them.

"Don't remove the newspaper, though."

"Mr. Blaiser, I can't soak them with the newspaper."

"But the newspaper is half the charm. Save the newspaper. Do you think you can rewrap the flowers properly?"

Her mouth fell open.

"Oh, never mind; I'll do it myself." He strode moodily to the magazine rack.

"It's the thought that accounts," she said, "not the newspaper."

"Or the flowers, or the fact that I'm here." He sat down heavily and became very busy reading *Coiffure Trends* upside down.

Angie shook her head.

★★★★★

The gallery, long and high-ceilinged, was cubicled off at intervals to achieve varied states of intimacy in which to view the art. One work, "Orgy at Nice," had nearly retired to one of these enclosures at the behest of the artist, but Jane had been adamant about its placement on a long wall. The circles and angles that crowded the canvas required space, breathing room. All wall space, enclosed and free, displayed splashes, blotches, dots or geometry alone or in company with one another. There were shapes, colors and subjects for all moods and tastes, one of Jane Blaiser's more eclectic art shows. The morning hours brought only a thin stream of people, and today was no exception. A young man with long hair stood before a mass of black encrustations and wrote in a notebook. A young couple stood at attention in front of a green tangle, and an elderly woman and her daughter gazed open-mouthed at "Orgy at Nice." Screened from view, except for her legs resting in sturdy squat shoes, visible at the bottom of a partition, was a young woman of indeterminate age and eyes of uncertain color. She wore a chunky brown coat and a tan woolen hat pulled over a head of golden-brown hair. There was a waif-like look about her face, not out of keeping with her ivory skin, but in sharp contrast to a steel-gray glint visible at intervals in her eyes. Perhaps it was the lighting. A small smile played on her lips as she gazed at the work before her: "Venus At Her Toilette. P. Terni. Oil on Cardboard."

"Do you approve?" Alan Blaiser addressed the back of her head. She did not turn. "I find it amusing," she said.

"Amusing? You find those black and brown contortions amusing? The triangular points of head, elbows and more private anatomical parts of the Goddess of Love amusing?"

Her laughter had the clarity and sweetness of a bell.

"Yes, I see what you mean." He laughed too. "Now Botticelli's Venus is my idea of the goddess, all delicacy and lightness and snake-like charm. Venus should be off limits to abstract art. She's flesh-and-blood illusion, not this."

"Woman is an abstraction, is she not? And Venus is the ultimate woman."

"But woman is flesh. No one thinks of Venus as a disembodied spirit. It's the flesh that matters."

"You sound hungry."

Alan laughed, but reddened. "How do you picture the goddess?"

A faraway look lit her eyes. "I don't picture her any way in particular."

"Got something against the Goddess of Love, have you?"

"Not at all. But mankind's preoccupation with her physical beauty often blinds it to the higher order of beauty she embodies."

"Mind over matter, eh? Somehow I don't believe that way of thinking about her will ever take hold."

The young woman smiled. "Don't you believe in the infinite beauty of spirit, the inexhaustible delights of love?"

Alan shifted legs awkwardly. "I can't see myself making love to my — to a woman's spirit. Look, I could use a cup of coffee right now. Why don't you join me? Then you can explain exactly what this is all about. I'm very open-minded; I'd like to learn."

She looked him full in the face. Her eyes were soft and the faint smile reappeared.

"Thank you, no." But she did not drop her eyes, and he felt an unbearable tension.

"Have you seen the 'Orgy'?" Alan blurted out.

They both burst into laughter.

★★★★★

In the crystal glassware sparkled the pink damask with which Jane had asked Penny to set the table. It was the round table upon which she and Alan dined once a month by candlelight. This was the second time that April that it had been so set, but the cloth was not the turquoise of the earlier date, nor was the candle the tall taper it had been before. Instead, it was a squat and chunky red, not the elegance Jane desired, but the festivity Alan preferred. The white drapes, side-tied in the afternoon, were drawn together now. Quite cozy and intimate, thought Jane with approval.

"Darling, what's this!" exclaimed Alan, as he skipped down the circular staircase of their duplex to the dining alcove below.

Jane removed a stem from the centerpiece and slipped it through his lapel as he stooped to kiss her.

"I assume I'd better cancel our dinner reservation."

"I already did," she said. "My surprise and my apology for this morning. Because I love you."

"You didn't have to go to this trouble. I was foolish this morning."

"Oh, darling, you're such a silly. It was no trouble. And you're never foolish."

"No, of course not. Bring on the hamburgers."

"Beef Stroganoff."

"And the apple pie."

"Apple dumplings."

"And Penny who loves me." Alan lifted his wine glass. "To Penny. And my wife who hired her."

"To love."

Alan pulled the stopper from the decanter and looked at the magenta swirls within for a long while before pouring the liquid, meeting Jane's glass above the center of the table, and downing the libation.

"Alan, what's the matter?"

"Nothing. Hard day, that's all."

"Are you sure, darling? We can talk about it," she offered.

Alan looked around at the trappings of romance and seemed about to say something. He knew that the unerringly accurate Jane sensed something was wrong. Otherwise, why would she be willing to break one of the rules of their monthly interludes — no business discussions? You couldn't fool Jane. He had never really wanted to.

"I met a beautiful girl in your gallery this morning," he said solemnly. "She looked a bit like this candle."

Jane choked with laughter, and Alan sprang to her side, thumping her on the back and begging her to raise her hands above her head.

"I'm all right," she gasped, still mirthful. "It's just a carryover from this afternoon. I was nearly in hysterics at lunch today. Even Maggie French was shocked. You see, *Flower Children* sent Vanessa. The dialogue went something like this:

'Why do you denigrate your flowers?'

'Why do I what?' Maggie was aghast.

'You bring out the symbolic worst in them. Why?'

Maggie was indulgent. 'Flowers have no personality and character of their own, other than what the beholder endows them with, and I've used traditional symbolism. I'm not a radical.'

'Why not? Think of all the delicious statements you could make if you were. You could discover the dandelion, take a brush to the cockscomb, display the naked beauty of the cactus, and let the dahlia in its various incarnations color the sun, moon, stars.'

'Now look here Miss —'

'Vanessa.'

'Miss Vanessa! My art, like all good art, reflects life. My viewers can identify with my flowers.'

'That's too bad, since you emphasize their negative attributes. Why must your roses and lilies be accompanied by thorns? Surely there is more to sunflowers than the agony of Van Gogh's conception, which you seem to admire. If you do not wish to show undiluted satisfaction, unalloyed fulfillment — quite a radical concept for mortals — why do you not at least show a balance? How do you expect to lift your audience higher?'

'I send the messages I receive. I'm sharing my view of flowers with others. I'm not trying to uplift anyone. Didactic art is the worst kind, and so are didactic reporters!'

Vanessa smiled sweetly. 'Do you like flowers?'

Maggie turned to me with a menacing growl.

'She's playing the devil's advocate with you,' I whispered. 'It's called aggressive reporting.'

Well, that mollified her somewhat, but it was all I could do to keep from doubling up with laughter. And Alan, Vanessa was such a sight! A dumpy-looking little thing with dark hair and big eyes. And clothes — like something out of *Vogue* 1940!"

Alan chuckled. "A provincial pedant in the big city. Poor kid. Probably her first assignment."

"And maybe her last, if Maggie has her way. She'd deserve it, too, unless she's kept on the payroll for comic relief. She's unreal."

"Just a country hick in a chunky brown coat, a kid with a porcelain complexion framed by a woolen hat."

"Darling," Jane exclaimed, as Penny entered with the appetizer. "You're exactly right! Oh, don't look so startled; it's a wonderful sign." She reached for his hands. "It means we're so close we can read each other's thoughts."

★★★★★

"We've run out of things to talk about, Dr. Schmeck. At our last tête à tête we were reduced to discussing the real world."

"And that is bad?"

"Alan is a romantic. Routine bores him. He must be able to escape periodically into storybook fantasy and adventure."

"These candlelit dinners are a regular feature each month?"

"Yes, doctor, I see what you mean. Even our romance has become routine. But what am I to do? Theoretically, creativity should be inexhaustible, so if I put my mind to it I suppose I could come up with an infinite number of ways to keep Alan amused, but I haven't the time."

"You found the time once, however?"

"Yes, before our marriage. But my situation was different then. I was a freelance artist, beholden to no one. Now I've got the gallery and a small but respectable reputation to uphold. Alan has his dad's business and workday commitments, so he should understand. But his business seems to run itself. Alan has no dream to fulfill."

"You wish to please him and to please yourself, and you see a conflict there."

"Not so much a conflict, doctor, more a lack of time and energy. If he were only a little more realistic ..."

"It would be more convenient."

"He would be happier," she countered.

"With whose reality? Yours? Mine? How do you define reality? Pragmatically? Subliminally? As the recognition of outer truths, inner truths or both? As the social and legal mores of a given era? You and your husband must find compatible definitions and share working them out or you must find more compatible mates."

Jane sat quite still. "Basically we share common ground," she faltered. "It's what attracted us to each other."

"But you have changed."

"I've grown. People grow. I don't believe they often really change what they are."

"Good point."

"I want Alan to grow, too."

"It would be convenient," the doctor repeated, puffing thoughtfully on his pipe. "Do you think you are outgrowing your husband?"

"I'm not sure I'll have the chance."

"Ménage a trois?"

"No," Jane said quickly. "At least, I don't think so. Not yet."

"But the possibility exists."

Jane looked toward the window. "It exists."

Dr. Schmeck uncrossed his legs and leaned forward to scrutinize her face. "There are certain signs you have seen?"

She gave a short, bitter laugh.

The doctor gave a few meditative puffs on his pipe. "I will not pretend to be able to help you, Mrs. Blaiser. I hope our little talk has helped you clarify the problem to better enable you to help yourself. Solutions can never be successfully imposed by a third party on any but robots. Your solution must come from within both of you. Should you be unable to successfully mesh your inner needs, you and your husband may wish to consult Dr. Fendrausen next door."

Jane looked bewildered.

Dr. Schmeck crossed the room and opened the door at the far end. "My next patient," he said, pointing to a man reclining in a chair, a dental drill overhead.

Jane's mouth opened wide.

"The mistake was yours," he said quickly, hastily shutting the door, "but you're neither the first to have made it, nor, I hope, the last. Misprints, confusion, reality! Actually, Dr. Fendrausen is too busy to screen potential clients, so it's really all to the good, and I don't charge. Frankly, I enjoy it. I must admit to a touch of boredom with teeth."

★★★★★

Jane was cross with herself for having spent her lunch hour with Dr. Schmeck, a man with an obvious penchant for mind over mouth. Yet, in a situation of trust, albeit false, she had allowed her mouth to reveal her mind. The interrelationship of functions! If only reality were romantic, but it went against the grain. Reality was, at best, interesting and challenging, and that was all. The fun and romance were superimposed on it, things of man's creating, palliatives to labor, boredom and pain. Mechanically, she waited for the light to change, then left the sidewalk for its duplicate across the street. The dentist was right. She would have to talk to Alan, to jointly find a way to meet her real and his romantic needs. An unreasonable emptiness settled in her stomach as she hurried back to the office, the faces in the street before her a geometric blur. She wasn't even aware she had brushed the shoulder of a woman who turned to watch her disappear down the street, a woman in a bulky, brown coat, her golden-brown hair burnished by a fortuitous ray of sun.

Chapter Two

THE HOUSE BEER SATISFYINGLY WASHED down the crusty bread and cheese. It had been a while since Alan had enjoyed such a munchy, crunchy meal. He was also enjoying the conversation of his luncheon companion.

"I'm delighted you don't always lecture," he said. "I was afraid you might criticize my choice of food or my eating habits."

"I can hardly do that, since I've followed your lead. Would you take criticism from a stranger?"

"From anybody who didn't really mean it. So you're a specialist in mythology, an expert in dreams. How delightful!"

She laughed. "If you ignore their bitter and bittersweet qualities. Daphne would have preferred to spend her time as a huntress rather than a tree, but she wished to avoid Apollo."

"Her father wished her to. Perhaps she would have thought better of it. Venus did all right by submitting. It didn't diminish her power, her self-respect or her appeal. If anything, it expanded and enhanced them."

"Venus was not a virgin goddess."

"I think Venus could be anything she wanted to be, every man's kind of woman, a woman for all places and all times, if she existed. But I'm glad she doesn't. I wouldn't know what to do with her!"

"Some situation would suggest itself, I'm sure. Perhaps you might bump into her, as you did me. You would invite her to join you for a sylvan repast in wooded surroundings — "

"With fake wooden beams — "

"But real butcher-block tables, and things would take care of themselves."

"You mean I'd only have to lean back and ohhh — ow!"

She reached both hands across the table to steady him, but in vain. She wound up with him on the floor, bread and cheese spiced with the haunting fragrance of beer sprinkled in their hair and on their clothes.

"Are you all right, Vanessa?"

"I'm fine, but I think you had better get to your feet with your back to the entrance. A friend of yours has just entered, and I don't think you would like him to see you here with me."

"Nonsense! I've nothing to hide. Businessmen have lunch with women all the time. Jane understands that. She lunches with men frequently herself."

"Jane?"

"A woman I know." He rolled to his knees and rose to his feet just as a heavyset man descended upon them. "Jack Gilbey, bane of my boyhood! How have you been?"

"Terrible," he said, straightening his shoulders and pulling in his middle paunch as far as it would go. "Won't you introduce me to your charming friend?"

"Oh, of course, of course. This is my wife Jane."

"There's nothing like having lunch with your wife, quite literally. But I'm glad to meet you anyway -uh- Jane." He took both her hands in his and shook them heartily. "Well, children, let's sit down! Alan, you look like the devil." He righted the chair for Vanessa and held it out for her. "Your lovely lady, though, looks like a nymph with forest garlands in her hair fresh from a nap under an oak tree amidst fallen leaves and flower pods and brush."

"Never married, I take it."

"Sharp, Alan, sharp. Most people are thrown by my middle. Think some wife's been feeding me. Actually," he said, patting his stomach, "this is full of poetry, song and humor plus, I'll admit it, as much beer as I can sneak in without losing my reputation. Few people know what is behind this facade of portly respectability, solidity and sense. Consider yourself honored."

"You went off to study law, as I remember. Did you stick with it?"

"Yes, indeed. You know I was never one to change my mind if I could help it. I'm out on the Coast now. Life is swimming along quite agreeably for me. All is sunny and steady, except for a few earth tremors now and then." He laughed robustly. "Excellent business, excellent." He smacked his lips.

"Lots of legal tangles out there?"

"Oh, lots. Tooth and claw type. Divorce law. Abounding in repeat business."

Alan rose. "It's really been wonderful seeing you after all these years," he said, his pleasure sounding hollow even to his own ears. He reached down for Vanessa's hands and drew her to her feet. "Back to work, darling."

"Alan! We've barely said hello. You're your own boss; you can set your own hours. You can't be so cruel as to walk out now!"

"Really, Jack. I've got a conference in fifteen minutes [he frantically pushed his sleeve up to get a glimpse of his watch], and Jane's got the gallery."

"I'm only in the city for the day. Our paths probably won't cross again for another fifteen years," he said shrewdly, Alan sat down.

"What's this about a gallery? I thought Jane was strictly the hausfrau type, or so the newspapers said, if I recall correctly."

Alan fidgeted with his beer stein. "That was Elaine. We were divorced almost seven years ago."

"Oh, sorry to hear it." His face fell. "But not very." He looked at Vanessa appreciatively.

"Wish you had let me know then. Not that I needed the business." Gilbey chuckled.

"What brings you to New York?" Alan asked with undue haste and interest.

"Business. Potential client distraught over a prospective divorce. Husband's been cheating on her. It may not mean divorce, but she's half worried that it will and half worried that it won't! It's all hush-hush. Her husband doesn't know she's decided to take action, and he mustn't know, at least not yet. There is no element as important in a war as the element of surprise."

"You must have quite a reputation to be sent for clear across the country," Alan said nervously.

His old chum looked serious. "That I do," he said quietly.

A warm feeling flooded Gilbey. It was of such intensity that he felt beads form on his face. He pulled a handkerchief from his pocket and dabbed at them. Alan made a mental note about the relationship between weight and perspiration.

Vanessa looked concerned. "Are you all right?"

"Yes, dear lady. A sudden flush." He blushed. "Ridiculous! Why don't you come with me, both of you," he said, his eyes meeting Vanessa's. "Jane can stay in the hotel lounge — they have impromptu entertainment from noon to two o'clock — and you can come with me as my associate to meet my client. For a lark, a change of pace."

"Divorce is no lark," Alan said solemnly, "and the change of pace concerns a subject I'd rather not contemplate."

"Of course," said Gilbey, "I understand. Still, seeing the woman's side, getting into her head, so to speak, might be - ah - useful. Real or imagined indiscretions may lead a spouse to take action, perhaps hasty and ill-conceived, but ..." He shrugged. "It can happen to any man, and a recurrence of the response may be avoidable."

"I did not cheat on Elaine. We found our lives drifting apart, so we divorced."

"How often have you seen her since this amicable breakup?"

"Unfortunately, our New York climate didn't agree with her. She left for New Mexico right after we signed the final papers."

"So sorry to hear it," Gilbey murmured, with just the trace of a smirk. "I hope she's well."

"I'm sure she is. Now I really must be getting back to the office."

"Alan, you won't mind if Mr. Gilbey drops me off later at the gallery, will you? I'd love to hear about your boyhood from a knowledgeable source. And perhaps, just perhaps, he will allow *me* to pose as his assistant and meet this poor lady. I think I would show more sympathy for her plight than he seems to have."

"Oh no, Jane, you misunderstand me. My dear, I have great sympathy and concern for this poor woman."

"And for her husband too, I suppose," Alan added wryly.

"For all concerned, for both parties, for myself. I have made the misfortunes of such people my life work, and it's a serious and sobering business, I assure you. I cannot part with you, both of you, having this wrong impression of me. You must come with me. Bother the gallery and the office! You must accompany me. I insist!"

"No," said Alan firmly. "Jane, I'm getting you a taxi."

"Alan, I'd really like to go with Jack."

Gilbey whipped out the handkerchief again.

"I said no. Don't argue with me."

Vanessa fixed him with a vacant stare, and a hollow feeling blew through Alan's frame.

"Of course, I can't forbid you," he amended gently. "I just thought your meetings, your appointments ..." He trailed off vaguely.

"Come with us, Alan," she beckoned. "Come." She helped the dazed Alan on with his coat, then turned her eyes to Gilbey. "You haven't eaten anything."

He dabbed at his face. "I'm not hungry, not at all."

Alan started. "What if this woman knows me or Jane?"

"She doesn't know anyone," said Gilbey absentmindedly. And they left.

Alan sat quietly in the taxi, his right arm protectively around Vanessa's shoulders. He half-listened to Gilbey's glib patter and Vanessa's wide-eyed innocent responses. Something about the capitals of the world compared to New York — theater, art, music and food. Gilbey, seated adjacent to the driver, turned his bulk to face Vanessa.

"Hasn't Alan taken you anywhere?" he asked in disbelief.

"I've been everywhere, but faraway places are forever exciting and new to me."

"Then New York City must bore you," Gilbey said, as the taxi lurched around a vehicle that had slowed for a turn and whizzed past landmarks.

"Not at all. New York *is* a faraway place."

"She means 'far out,'" Alan injected hastily.

"Is that what you mean?" queried Gilbey curiously.

"Yes."

"Hmmm. You've ingested Shakespeare's *Shrew*, I see."

Vanessa laughed. "You are incorrigible, as are all men."

"Incorrigible, are we? And why do you think that?"

"No particular reason," she replied in a small voice, as she huddled closer to Alan.

Alan bit his lower lip, and it felt warm and moist.

"You knew," he said hoarsely, not daring to look at her. "You knew Jack and I were friends."

"But you said so."

"That was after. You knew at once."

Vanessa smiled. "I am a woman. And time is of no consequence to me."

As Alan turned to look at her, a sharp light caught his left eye, causing him to throw his head back in pain.

His companion ran whisper-soft palms across his face, over his eyelids and his brows.

"Close your eyes, darling," she breathed.

Alan swallowed hard, his eyes shut, his arms holding Vanessa.

With some anxiety, Gilbey surveyed the silent pair in the mirror.

"Just another block," Vanessa noted.

Gilbey half turned around. "You know the place?"

A mischievous twinkle lit her eyes, but she said evenly, "I've read the script."

"And what do you think of it?" queried Gilbey.

"More than you will, I'm afraid."

Gilbey was still puzzling that one out as he handed the young woman out of the taxi, preventing Alan from performing the gallantry, the taxi having stopped on the wrong side of the street to allow Alan the privilege.

"Thinking of making this building a landmark," said Gilbey, jerking a thumb toward the decaying facade.

"Who's thinking?" asked Alan darkly.

"Landmark Commission, of course."

Gilbey steered them to a sofa with its back facing the reception desk, firmly seated them, placed their hands in each other's and stalked decisively toward the desk clerk. Alan swiveled his head to follow Gilbey's movement. When his face met Vanessa's once more it was full of suspicion and foreboding.

"It's all right, Alan. There's nothing sinister about Jack. The silly man likes me. You're not going to fault his taste now, are you?"

"Of course not. But that silly man can get you into trouble that will make your head spin. I don't want you hurt. You're staying close to me. No mid-day bistro pickup for you. You wanted to come here. All right! But I want to make sure that nothing unpleasant happens to you. And I will!"

"Because I went along with the Jane charade or because you like me?"

"Because, like Jack, I've been acting like a silly ass. Only I know it."

"'Silly' comes from an Old English word meaning 'happiness' ", mused Vanessa. "I think silly people are rather appealing."

Alan looked surprised. "Jane thinks so, too. Only I wish her behavior were based a little less on thinking and a little more on feeling."

Gilbey approached them. "Now Jane, my dear, we'll deposit you safely in the Music Lounge. Then Alan and I will attend to this business. I know, I know. You want to come with us, but you'll get the sordid story filtered through Alan's most capable mind. Now, you mustn't look at me that way. It's best for you, believe me, isn't it Alan?"

"Hard to say until I know who you've got lined up for her in there."

"Well, I did see an old friend of mine about to start his dessert. I just glanced in to make sure the place was suitable for an attractive, married young woman. Luckily, I saw this friend. No competition, no danger at all. Extremely safe. No need to worry, Alan. He's a friend."

"Of *yours*. No need to worry at all."

Vanessa rose, moved gracefully toward the desk clerk, paused for a moment's conversation and the acquisition of a steno pad and pencil, and floated toward the elevator. Alan and Jack looked at each other blankly, then scrambled after her.

★★★★★

The woman said she was pleased to meet Mr. Blaiser and Miss Brownley. She was somewhere in her forties with deep rings under her eyes. Touches of pencil had made her tweezed brows a match to her black hair., which waved around her face. Her figure was tentatively slim. The room was a small one, and the upholstery was worn. The window faced some pipes and a wall.

"I didn't want to be conspicuous," she apologized. "Would you like a scotch and soda?" she asked brightly. "I'll ring for more glasses."

"Mrs. Munson, sit still, dear lady, relax. The drink is of no importance."

"But you've come all this way for me."

Alan felt his face redden, despite the sickly yellow light. He turned his gaze toward the window.

Mrs. Munson, with much kneading of hands, explained her distress: the psychological, social and financial repercussions for her of a divorce, and the continuing damage to her self-esteem and a possible public loss of face should she choose to ignore the infidelity and come to terms with her husband.

"Dear lady, you cannot have it both ways."

"I know that," she said with feeling. Wide-eyed, she scanned his face. "Which way is better, do you think?"

"My dear, I can custom-tailor a settlement to meet your wishes, whichever choice you make, but I cannot make that choice for you."

She nodded and heaved a deep sigh. "Miss Brownley, what would you do?"

"Mrs. Munson, you are being unfair," interjected Gilbey. "You're putting Jane in a terrible position. What would you have her say?"

"What she will."

"Only you can answer your question," insisted Gilbey.

"But I need advice." She turned to Jane. "Are you married?"

"Yes."

"Then it's *Mrs.* Brownley. You should have corrected me, Mr. Gilbey. Mrs. Brownley," she repeated, and was silent for a moment. "Are you happy, Jane Brownley. Is your marriage happy?"

"Yes to both questions."

"It's one question, only one question. You really must be happy or you would know that. I'm sorry you're happy, Mrs. Brownley. It sounds unkind, I know, but I'm sorry."

"Very, very sorry?"

Mrs. Munson smiled. "Call me Adele."

"Adele, Shakespeare said that all the world's a stage, and all the men and women merely players. Perhaps —"

"Oh, literature, rubbish!"

"I beg your pardon!" said Vanessa with mock outrage. "We are the stuff of literature, and we will be around for as long as there is time, and maybe even longer. At least I will."

Adele Munson smiled again. "Me too. You were saying?"

21

"That perhaps role-playing would help you decide on the best course of action. You would play yourself, I could play the other woman, and Mr. Gilbey could play Mr. Munson."

"Oh no, no. I'll have nothing to do with it. Casting me in the scoundrel's role! Really, Jane!"

"You could pretend," urged Adele Munson.

"But I've never been married!"

"Do you deny ever having acted the scoundrel?"

"I most certainly do, Jane! This is all nonsense. We've lost sight of the problem completely!"

"I haven't. I want you to be my lawyer and I want you to pretend. I'm paying you and paying well."

Gilbey looked at Alan helplessly.

Adele Munson searched Vanessa's eyes. "But first, if you would," she asked almost shyly, "I'd like an answer to my question. What would you do?"

"If I were to find myself in your position, Adele Munson, I should laugh," she responded seriously.

"Laugh!" echoed Mrs. Munson.

"Laugh!" affirmed Vanessa.

"Mrs. Munson," said Gilbey gently, "perhaps another look at the benefits and liabilities of the various alternatives you can command now, before the initiative is lost …"

"I can always laugh."

"My dear Mrs. Munson, you don't need the services of a lawyer to laugh. You must not allow emotion to color your reason. Don't forget your children."

"Why not? They seem to have forgotten me. They're too busy with their own silly social problems. Irresponsible and spoiled. Daddy's angels. Daddy's generosity knows no limits. He gives his favors lavishly." She burst into tears.

"My dear, my dear, you mustn't! You're breaking my heart!" Gilbey uttered in an anguished voice, as he put an arm around the heaving shoulders of Adele Munson and cast despairing eyes on a starched shirt front rapidly turning damp and limp. "There, there," he said, massaging her back. "I'm here to help you. Together we'll set things to rights, you and I, but you mustn't cry. If our role-playing is to bear fruit you must dry your eyes. Here," he said, reaching for the handkerchief in his breast pocket.

She stifled convulsive sobs and allowed him to dab her eyes.

"If I play your husband and as your husband I see tears, my response to you would be, at the least, slightly dishonest, at the most, sheer fabrication. There now, that's better. Well," he said with resignation, "shall we begin? Alan you will be our objective observer and impartial analyst. Take notes." Jack Gilbey thrust Jane's pad and pencil at him, then cleared his throat. "Adele — may I call you that? — begin."

She clasped her hands in front of her. "I don't quite know how," she confessed.

"How about reimagining the specific time you felt impelled to question Mr. Munson about his extra-marital activities," suggested Gilbey.

She looked flustered. "That was in bed the night of our last anniversary. I don't think I could —"

"No, no, of course not. Jane, what would you suggest? It was your idea."

"Adele, is there anything about Mr. Gilbey that reminds you of your husband — his eyes, his hair, his hands, his build — anything you can fasten your attention on?"

"I wouldn't have hired him if he in any way resembled my husband. My husband is a tall, good-looking man, independent, alive. His hair is thinning somewhat, but most of it is still dark, and it rather complements his trim figure. I can still be objective even if he - we- get divorced."

Alan scribbled "independent, alive … objective."

"Alan, my boy," Gilbey beamed. "You were made for the part!"

"Oh, no," said Mrs. Munson. "He looks too young."

"But," pursued Gilbey, "your husband feels young when in the company of his, uh, female companions. Pretend that's what you see in Alan."

"No, I won't do it, Jack! You're going too far. You —"

"Alan, Alan, control yourself. These outbursts are not your prerogative. *You're* not getting divorced again."

"Again?" uttered Mrs. Munson as though she had been struck.

"And furthermore," continued Gilbey, "if you refuse to cooperate, I'll fire you on the spot!"

"Wonderful!" It came out savagely "Come on, Jane!"

"Just a moment," thundered Gilbey. "Where do you think you are going with my secretary?"

"My God! My husband all over," Mrs. Munson declared in awe.

"If you think I'll let her stay here with you, you're crazy."

"Perhaps we should ask Jane that," said Gilbey. "Jane, my dear?"

Vanessa fixed them both with an enigmatic smile. "I think someone should answer the door."

"I didn't hear anything," said Adele Munson.

There was a knock on the door.

"But no one knows I'm here," Adele responded to Jack Gilbey's lifted eyebrows.

"I'll get it, then," he said, rising.

"No! I will. It's my life. I must begin to take charge of it."

Gilbey noted the neat turn of her hips as she walked toward the door.

The opened door revealed a man leaning against the door moulding, a tall, gaunt man with gray brushed through his hair. He hiccuped and nearly fell backward.

"Adele, whycha change? I told you I'd be right back." He held the door frame with both hands to steady himself.

"I don't know this man," Mrs. Munson called over her shoulder. Her eyes snapped at the intruder. "Go away!"

"Aw, now cmon … ow! Whatcha do that for?"

24

"You had no business sticking your foot in my door. I don't know you. Now go away!"

The man hopped like a wounded bird, then hiccuped and fell forward onto Mrs. Munson and into the room.

Jack and Alan looked at each other, rose from their seats, and ranged themselves on either side of the prostrate man. They took hold of him under the armpits and moved him toward the door.

"Hey! Whatszis?"

"You've made a mistake, buddy," said Alan.

"Nah, you've made the mistake. Tell them, Adele."

But Adele said nothing. Her eyes were big with apprehension and her hands covered her mouth. She shrank back as the intruder was carried past her. Jack Gilbey glowered at her under his eyebrows, but the stranger took resolution and strength from her expression, made more poignant by the blur of his double vision.

"Get your hands offa me. I'm not leavin' Adele."

His knees became rubber. As he was pulled to his feet, he grabbed one each of his assailants' legs. "Don't worry, honey. I'll save ya, I'll save ya."

Adele Munson watched in dismay. The stranger's strength was amazing, considering his drunken condition and his haggard appearance. Avoiding the scramble of bodies on the floor, she edged her way to the door.

"Oh, my!" she exclaimed to no one in particular.

In the hallway were the hurrying figures of men and women in various states of dishabille. The stairs on opposite ends of the hall and the set of elevators in the center were attracting them like magnets.

"What is it? What's happening?" she shouted at a woman running past, her shoes in her hands.

"Run for your life!" was the shouted reply.

"My God, my God! Jack! Alan! Jane! We've got to get out of here!" she screamed into the room. "There's a fire!"

"You can say that again," said a grim-faced man, his tie flapping out of his jacket pocket as he hurried by. "Cops!"

Adele Munson had no time to absorb this information. Two men were shoved past her into the oncoming traffic, a hand reached out for her and pulled her into the room, and the door slammed shut. The two looked at each other for a moment.

"You're not my Adele."

"No."

"But those men were bothering you."

"They weren't bothering me. They're my friends."

"Both of them?"

"Friends, like human beings. Do you know what human beings are?" she asked with irritation.

"Yes," he said mournfully. "I used to know some, used to be one myself." He shook his head as though to clear it.

"I don't have any coffee, and I'm afraid Room Service will not send any for a while."

Commands, whistles and shrieks could be heard beyond the paper-thin walls of the room.

"The police?"

"Yes."

"Then we'll be together for a while longer," he said. "Do you mind? My name is George."

Chapter Three

JANE CHEWED ON THE END of her pencil. Her left elbow rested on the desk, her left hand pressed against her temple. She had met him seven years ago at the Treeley Ball. Her cheeks had been softer then, her skin unlined. In those days she had kept her eyeglasses in their case rather than where they belonged, and she could truly say that physical appearance did not weigh strongly in her choice of men. She had gone with Eric Ludwig, her agent until his retirement five years ago when she took over his business and started the gallery. She smiled at the recollection of his chest ready to burst out of the tux, the bow tie kept askew by his second chin, and the cherubic face, serene, secure, in constant motion. Dear, sweet, wonderful Eric! How often he had scolded her for neglecting her social life. Perspective, he had said. Perspective in life as well as in art.

Make your life a work of art; there is room for the canvas in it, too. And she had hugged him, kissed his balding head, and made a date that very weekend with one of a seemingly endless stream of unsuitable marriage prospects just to make him happy. He had escorted her to the Treeley Ball and judiciously maneuvered her around the pink and white chandeliered ballroom on the ground floor of the Treeley estate and into conversations with men he thought might catch her fancy. She laughed aloud and dropped the pencil. There was the rug man, tall Ralph Riley, because Jane was tall, and short, bushy-haired Matt Grell, because Jane did not like rugs.

There was scholarly John Bottnell, because Jane admired a brilliant mind, and toe-tapping Phil Fussey, because Jane was an excellent dancer. And then, totally unbidden, a tall man with a friendly face was asking her to dance and whisking her across the floor, making all faces but his own a blur and welding all colors into pastel glitter and light. Alan, Alan Blaiser! She was airborne and free in the arms of Prince Charming while Elaine Treeley Blaiser surely looked on, surely foresaw the loss of that sweet-faced, silly romantic she had married when she was a dewy eighteen, and for whom she had found increasingly less time ever since. Beginnings. So exciting, so dreadful. Eric was not pleased. He frowned on her business luncheons with Alan, her business cruise with Alan. The man obviously had no interest in art. She bristled. She still had that watercolor of the waves washing over the side of a dinghy he had painted just for her, his first artistic effort. Eric had thought her better disciplined, disciplined to do what was right rather than what she liked. She had replied that experimentation involved a discipline of its own, but he had shaken his head. You do not discipline a butterfly. You do not change it back into a caterpillar. And she had not. She looked around the office. If it were Alan or this, which would she choose? She couldn't make that choice; she wouldn't. She would wind up with nothing.

She got up, walked to the window, pushed it open, and leaned out. Honking horns drowned out her thoughts, and the patchwork movement below replaced the unnerving image of a boyish, smiling Alan.

"Nice, huh?"

She looked up.

"Top of the day, ma'am! Mrs. Blaiser, right?"

"Yes," she said faintly. She rallied. "Top of the day to you, too."

"Now, that's the ticket! Mind if I wash your window now?" He lowered the scaffold.

"Have you finished the windows above?"

"Nah. Finish them later. A gentleman always makes a detour for a pretty lady."

"You won't get far in life if you don't finish what you start."

"Already been far and didn't like it. Now take that lamp place. No law says it has to be done right away. Staring into all those artificial lights hurts the eyes."

"A good excuse."

"Thank you," he said cheerfully. "I thought so, too."

"Well, I won't keep you from your work." She walked back to her desk and started fussing with the papers on it. She was really finished for the day. If Alan surprised her with a visit now, she could enjoy it. Bills paid, accountant seen, interviews completed, invitations to the Trumbull opening night in the mail. What more was there to do today? She moved uncomfortably in her chair. She hated to be idle. Doing anything, even washing windows, was better than doing nothing. She was suddenly aware of a prickly sensation and cold arms. She turned toward the window. The stocky young man sat on his haunches and was smiling at her through the open window.

"Just what do you think you are doing?"

"Resting, ma'am."

"Well, that's your business, but would you mind shutting the window? It's barely spring!"

"Never guess it from all the flowers lining the walls of your gallery, even if they are a bit hard to make out."

"You've seen the show?"

"Yes, ma'am. I'm in it. I'm the cherub in 'Heaven Looks at Man's Abominations and Sighs.' You know, the angles topped with curly hair?"

"Won't you come in, Mr. Cherub? You may as well rest inside."

"Thank you, ma'am, but no. It wouldn't look right. Man coming through your window and all. Got to live up to my painting." He closed the window.

Jane pulled a scratch pad toward her and furiously began to sketch an angel sitting on a cloud. He had buck teeth, unfocused eyes, a pointy nose, and a pair of horns. She turned toward the window, but the cherub was gone. She ripped the sketch from the pad, crumpled it into a ball, and threw it into the wastebasket. Then she leaned her head on the desk. She lay quietly for a few moments before reaching for a button on her intercom.

"Angie, I'm leaving now. Oh, that can wait until tomorrow. Close up, will you?" She turned at the door to put on her coat. The office looked so dreary, so dead. She smiled and flicked off the light. Wouldn't Alan be surprised to see her!

★★★★★

"What is it, Mr. Blaiser?"

"I'd like to see one of the girls you apprehended at the hotel, Miss — Sergeant."

"This is a police station, not a brothel. If that is all —"

"No, you don't understand —"

Sergeant Weller waved a hand at him impatiently. "You want to see one of the ladies of the night we caught during our daylight raid today, and I'm telling you the answer is no."

"But she must be badly frightened. She was picked up by mistake. She was with me."

"And, I take it, your apprehension was a mistake?"

"Very definitely a mistake! I went to the hotel with a lawyer to see a lady on strictly legitimate business. We weren't with those others."

"Uh huh, uh huh. You will have your say in court, Mr. Blaiser; you can explain it all then. I take it you have phoned your lawyer —"

"I don't need a lawyer! I'm innocent!"

"And will be provided with bail."

"Yes."

"So there is nothing further to say."

"There is something further to say, and you will listen to me!" He petulantly stamped his right foot on the floor.

"Mr. Blaiser, really!"

"Sergeant Weller, you're a woman."

"You noticed."

"Sergeant, I find nothing humorous about this."

"You're right. Continue."

"Look at me. Do I look like the kind of man who would run after women?"

She opened her mouth.

"In broad daylight on a business day?" he added hastily. "Look at my appointment calendar." He yanked a memo pad from his jacket pocket. "I haven't got time for women today, even if I wanted to see any, which I don't! Look!" He thrust the pad at her.

She kept her hands folded on the desk. "Mr. Blaiser, I'm not your judge, and I haven't got time for this. Save it for later, will you?"

"But this girl," he persisted. "You're a woman —"

"I'm a police sergeant."

"But you're also a woman; you can't deny it!"

Sergeant Weller sighed. "What is this girl's name?"

"Jane Brownley."

"Jane Brownley." She thumbed through a book on the desk. "We don't have a Jane Brownley in custody. Try another name," she said wryly.

He wet his lips. "Maybe if I could look at the book myself?"

Sergeant Weller rose. "Mr. Blaiser —"

"All right, all right. Do you have anyone with dark hair and a pretty face? She was wearing a brown coat."

"Well, that description narrows it down quite a bit. Perhaps if we paraded the dozen of them in front of you we could determine her identity."

"Oh, would you?" he asked hopefully. "I'd be so grateful."

"Guard, return Mr. Blaiser to his cell."

"But Sergeant Weller, this is serious. She's never been in jail before. Sergeant — !"

Sergeant Weller shook her head. "Men!"

★★★★★

31

The air blew through her hair and gave her the sensation that with little effort she could float. She was touched with that special blend of harmony and excitement that filled her at this time of year. She laughed inwardly. Was it about now, eons ago, that she supposedly had risen from the sea? Her eyes moved unseeing past the mannequins and other hardware of life, circa 1980. She loved the sea and the sky, and the endless, ageless cycle of birth and rebirth of all in-between — trees and flowers, mountains and valleys, all manner of four-legged creatures and man, generic anomaly for without her sex, unabashedly acknowledged, where would man or his "kind" be? The lilting of the turtledove came to her from the East and the twittering of the companionable swallow from the Coast. The displays in the store windows as examples of some sort of desirable opulence and the mobile figures wrapped up in the twentieth century were but passing visions, substantial, yet unreal. It had always been so. Through the curtains of circular time blew spring, its kernel an individual discovery, its superficial manifestation an event that could never be imposed by fashion or by will. Even the ram had never been able to force compliance with human expectations on March 20. The natural world went its own way. She was almost sorry she had come. Her spirit could have traveled well enough. But she had chosen to attend to this affair herself, and so she would. She pushed the revolving doors and entered Lord & Taylor, a world of crystal and silver. And she was in a hundred ballrooms, dancing with dukes and kings, dining on sumptuous fare, and enjoying the visual results, both horrific and delightful of haute couture's encasing and disguise of the real thing. She took pleasure in making her selections. There were potential uniforms of varied composition — severe linen, perishable silk, chiffon, satin, lace and brocade. And masks, preposterously solemn, silly, sanguine masks. The credit card she found after some rummaging in her bag was accepted without question. Jane did not need it just now. At a thought, it would be with her again. Well done, she told herself, as she revolved her way out of the store. A bolt of lightning lit the street. Vanessa smiled up at the sky. People quickened their pace. Some raised their coats or newspapers to cover their heads, while others scurried for cover. A drizzle had begun, but soon the rain was pouring down in sheets. Foolish to be rushing or hiding, thought Vanessa. Rain is so nourishing, so cleansing. She strolled down Fifth Avenue as though she were taking a turn in the sun, her hair dripping, her face shining and wet. I do so love the rain, she thought.

★★★★★

"Thanks, Digby."

"Not at all, Mr. Blaiser," said Digby, helping him off with his wet coat.

"I know I can count on your discretion. Stupid mistakes like this can cause no end of trouble. Thank goodness no reporters were there."

"Yes, sir. Why don't you stretch out on the sofa in your office. I'll bring some coffee there in a few minutes."

"Thanks. I can use some."

Digby had just put the coffee into the pot when an insistent buzz from the chief's office captured his attention.

"Digby here."

"Digby," said the voice with forced calm, "come in here immediately."

Digby, short, efficient, quick was in the office before Alan had finished speaking. Alan stood at the open door to his closet. He was not wearing his jacket or tie, and the hand extending out of his creased shirt sleeve pointed at the closet.

"I wanted my robe!" Alan exploded.

"Of course, sir, and here it is." Digby took the worn, blue-striped terry from its hanger and held it out for Alan.

"I don't want it!" Alan swept it from Digby's hands and onto the floor. "What the hell is this?"

"Why, some lady's apparel," said Digby, somewhat confused.

"I know that, you dummy, but whose?"

"I have no idea, sir. You didn't place them here?"

"No, I did *not* place them here," said Alan testily, "and I want to know who did!"

"They weren't here this morning when I checked the office. Did you happen to look in your closet when you arrived, sir?"

Alan clasped his hands to his head and roared.

"Then," concluded Digby, "since the staff well knows that your office is entered by invitation only, and since such invitations are issued only by you or by me, in your absence, I would assume that these female garments were delivered during my absence, while I was attending to the correction of your, uh, mishap. I will certainly make inquiries into the matter immediately, sir."

"You certainly will *not* make inquiries! That's all I need, to have this thing blabbed throughout the building. And if Jane hears about this … This day is turning into a nightmare!"

"May I suggest that these clothes may be Mrs. Blaiser's? Perhaps she is planning a little interlude and wants to surprise you."

"Not Jane, not during office hours, and these aren't her clothes."

"Perhaps she bought some new things," Digby said helpfully. He pulled out a few. "My, my, quite sexy, sir! Could she be planning a night out and wish to change in your office?"

"She only did that once, and then she changed in *her* office." An agitated Alan strode up and down the room.

"Oh, sir," said Digby brightly, "do you know an A.W.?"

"An A.W.?" repeated Alan blankly.

"Yes, sir. Her label is in several of the garments."

"Those are the designer labels."

"Beg your pardon, but they're not, sir."

"Let me see!" He was back at the closet in a leap. "By golly, you're right! And they're in all these things!"

"Think, sir. You must know an A.W."

"Damn it, Digby, I don't, but I expect you to, and before the end of this day! Be discreet, you must be absolutely discreet, but find out who this A.W. is and how her clothes got into my closet. Maybe they were delivered to the wrong office," he said hopefully.

"They were probably meant for Don Byron," Digby said consolingly.

"Yes, yes, that's probably it. Thank you, Digby."

"Shall I also check on the ownership of the little items? There are no personal labels in them."

Looped through a hanger on which hung one of Alan's spare shirts, were a set of female underthings.

"With all due respect, sir, perhaps somebody is trying to tell you something."

"Get out!" shouted Alan. "Get out," he repeated in a hoarse whisper, "and get to work on this!" He pointed to his closet as he kicked it shut with his foot. "Oh, I've got to lie down!"

Jane crossed the lobby of Blaiser and Son without attracting more than an admiring glance from a male who chanced to look up from his desk. She drew no recognition from Alan's employees, and merited none. She hadn't been to the building above several times during their six-year marriage, and in their determined effort to separate business from pleasure, she and Alan had never attended business parties together. She took the elevator to the fourth floor. Unlike the floors below it was narrow, accommodating only the offices of the company's division leaders and the president.

Digby emerged from Alan's office, saw Jane the instant she saw him, and looked like he was about to have a stroke. Arwood Digby was Alan's personal assistant and alter ego. Perhaps she was intruding.

"Mr. Digby," she began. She hated to call him Digby, as though he were still the valet Alan had raised to executive status, and Arwood was too informal. "Mr. Digby, will I be in the way? Is Alan too busy for me?"

"Good gracious, no," said Digby nervously. "Mr. Blaiser would drop whatever he was doing to see you, if he were doing anything. But he's not, you see, so he won't be able to, I'm afraid."

"Say that again? No, never mind. I'll just go in and surprise him," she said, moving past him.

"Shock," he said, jumping in front of the door to Alan's office and barring the way. "It would be a shock, uh, he's had a shock, a nasty shock, electric, and he's resting just now."

"My poor darling! When did this happen?"

"Suddenly, very suddenly."

"Is he all right? Oh, but I must see him!"

"No, no, you mustn't. Mr. Blaiser made a special point about it. He doesn't want you to see him like this."

"Mr. Digby, will you please step aside?"

"But he's sleeping!" pleaded Digby.

"Is my husband having an affair in there at this moment?"

"Oh, no! Heaven forbid!"

"Is he eating potato salad in defiance of the diet he's on?"

"Certainly not."

"Did he rehang that ghastly portrait of his mother over his desk?"

"Not at all, I assure you."

"Then he'll want to see me."

"I can't allow it madam!"

"Oh, Arwood, you look so handsome, and gallant, and strong standing there like that!"

She tried to throw her arms around him, but that vigilant and agile man quickly stepped aside to avoid her embrace. She was in Alan's office in a flash.

"Darling, are you all right?"

Alan sat bolt upright. "Jane, what are you doing here?"

"I couldn't help it, sir," said Digby weakly from the door, which he quietly closed.

She sat beside him on the sofa. "Digby told me you had a terrible shock. You poor dear! How did it happen?"

"I don't know. How do such things happen? We were doing what we felt was right, in all innocence, and we were raided! Would you believe it? I was mortified! They wouldn't listen to reason!"

"Alan, what on earth are you talking about?"

"But didn't Digby — ?"

"He told me you'd had an electric shock!"

"Good old Digby," said Alan faintly. "The truth is we were raided. And it certainly was a shock!"

"Where?"

"Here, of course. Right out from under our noses. One of our best men. That's what makes me so sick. I wanted him to replace Byron when he leaves. No one else we've got would be as good."

"Well, I'm relieved to hear it's only business. Your Mr. Digby was horrid to scare me with that electric shock story."

"Well," he laughed, likewise relieved, "I guess Digby thought you'd rather hear that I'd suffered an electric shock than that I'd had a nervous breakdown."

"You'll get over it, darling," she said soothingly, her arms around his neck.

"I suppose, in time, but I'm sore as hell about it. It's hard to run a successful business that way. This company can't live on yesterday's achievements. We can't even afford to keep up with the times. We've got to move ahead of them. And damn it, that means attracting and keeping the best minds we can find in the business!"

Jane had never heard Alan speak so passionately about business. It almost made her glad about the raid. "This company, what's its name?"

"Munson," he said quickly.

"Well, these Munson thieves must be pretty desperate to practically pull this man off the premises. They're probably no match for Blaiser & Son."

"They *did* pull him off the premises," said Alan with growing assurance. "It was like a grade B movie script. Apparently, advancement was not as important to him as an outsized salary. Raiders like Gilbey should be arrested! Barging onto private premises to steal and refusing to leave!"

"You should have called the police. The man was trespassing."

"That was my first thought, but I — " The intercom buzzed.

"Sergeant Weller is here to see you."

"— But it took this long for them to send somebody around. Our efficient police department!" He turned to the intercom. "Digby, see my wife out and have Sergeant Weller come in, please."

"And I was hoping we could have a lovely little interlude. Well, darling, I tried." Jane kissed her husband and headed for the door.

Digby ushered Sergeant Weller in as Jane made her exit, delayed by a split-second expression of surprise as she surveyed the incoming policewoman.

Alan's heart sank for a moment. What explanation would Digby provide for the looks of Sergeant Weller? Indeed, what explanation would Sergeant Weller provide?

"You're not in uniform, Sergeant. Don't you realize how frightening that can be?"

"Most people find my uniform more frightening than my person, Mr. Blaiser," she said, amused.

"People can get the wrong idea. My wife hears you announced as a sergeant, and you enter as a woman."

"Mr. Blaiser, I have no identity crisis. If you do, I'm sorry for it," she said evenly. "You left one of your cuff links at the station house. Since I have an engagement nearby, I thought I would deliver it."

"Trailing a suspect, I take it, requires a plainclothes outfit."

"I'm off-duty now, Mr. Blaiser," she responded stiffly.

She looked anything but stiff, Alan noted. Her hair, which had been tied in a bun at the back of her head earlier in the day, now hung softly around her face and fell onto the shoulders of a scoop-necked, long-sleeved blue crepe dress, which effectively molded an excellent figure. Her face, which had appeared hawkish and hard under the severe hairdo, now appeared soft and inviting. Her legs were good, too.

"How did you know the cuff link was mine?"

"You shook it at me several times."

"But you were unshakable."

"One must not be shaken by situations. It impedes one's ability to react sensibly to them. In my job this trait is especially important."

"It's not human nature to remain calm under all circumstances, but perhaps a uniform helps perpetuate that trait in those so inclined."

"Your cuff link, Mr. Blaiser." She placed it on the palm of his hand.

"I didn't mean to upset you."

"I'm not upset."

"Well, you should be. I'm sorry. Uh, nothing personal, but — what size dress are you wearing?"

"I beg your pardon."

"Your dress. I like the size of it for my wife. What size is it?"

Sergeant Weller laughed. She had lovely teeth. "Eight," she said, forcing her face back into composure. "Good day, Mr. Blaiser."

"Wait a minute!" he yelled desperately. "Look, I'm sure you must be in a rush, but — do you have any identification on you?"

She turned to face him squarely. "Mr. Blaiser, what is it you want?"

"Your first name."

"Incubus."

"Sergeant, you barge into my office without proper identification —"

"Well, I'm barging right out, so calm yourself. I've done my good deed for the day."

"No, you haven't. Not unless you answer my question. I think I may have something of yours. It's just a crazy feeling."

"Mr. Blaiser, you may be crazy, but I doubt if you have any real feeling for anyone, and you can have nothing that belongs to me."

"Then you won't show me your police identification?"

"That is correct."

"Isn't there anything I can do to persuade you?"

"No, you've done your best."

Alan looked on helplessly as she made her exit. Suddenly, he pounced on the telephone."

"Digby!" he commanded. "Digby, what's the weather forecast?" he asked in a precipitous change of tone.

"I'll find out sir, and get back —"

"And the tides, Digby; find out about the tides."

"But sir —"

"No buts about it. A little sea air is just what I need. Do wonders for me. Is she gone?"

"What? Oh, yes, sir. But the sea —"

"Forget the sea. Follow her!"

"The sea, sir?"

"No, you idiot! Sergeant Weller!"

"But where did she go?"

"If you'd follow her maybe you'd find out! She's got a date somewhere in the neighborhood. Now get going, and don't let her see you."

Digby was too forlorn to say "yes, sir." He heaved a sigh of resignation, grabbed his umbrella, and made a dash for the door.

Chapter Four

"DARLING, YOU LOOK BEAUTIFUL." THE tall, curly-haired man *clasped* her hands in his. "You hang upon the cheek of night like a rich jewel in an Ethiop's ear."

"It's hardly night yet, Don."

"I'm anticipating, feverishly anticipating."

"Then it's not beauty too rich for use, for earth too dear?" she said, continuing the *ROMEO & JULIET* motif.

"Oh, Ann, if you'd only trust me and trust yourself we'd both end up —"

"Dead."

"In heaven."

"That's what I said."

"This police work has spoiled you for all the beauty in life. For the nth time, Ann, I beg you, leave it behind and marry me."

"I thought we decided to let the subject rest for a bit."

"I'm sorry, darling, but whenever I see you I'm just so overwhelmed."

Ann Weller nodded and smiled faintly. "And I can never understand why," she murmured.

"You don't see yourself as I do."

"Apparently not. Are we ordering?"

"With all deliberate speed. Ambrosia is not on the menu. We shall have to settle for more mortal delights: Chicken à la Queen, Keats Lorraine — I love you Ann."

"Beef Bourguignon," she said, her eyes watering.

★★★★★

"I don't know why I'm having dinner with you."

"Try not to think about it; you'll enjoy it more."

"Is that the game you're playing? That's all it is, you know."

The man winced.

"I'm sorry, George. I shouldn't have said that."

"No, you're right, Adele. It's the easy way, the less painful way. When I think, I try to thrash it all out, why Lucy doesn't love me anymore."

"Your other women couldn't have helped."

"Is that why you left your husband?"

"I haven't left him yet."

"Will you?"

"I don't know."

"You're a good woman, Adele. That's not just flattery. I mean it," he said mournfully.

"Thank you, George, but you must get a grip. All this mooning about and feeling sorry for yourself isn't helping you a bit."

"I'm lost, Adele. I've ruined my life. A wonderful woman has turned her back on me, and my kids don't want to know me."

"Your kids, as you call them, are married with families of their own. They don't have to know you. It would be nice, for them as well as you, but it's not necessary. As for your wonderful wife, well, maybe she was too wonderful."

"I resent that, Adele, I really do. Lucy doesn't deserve criticism. I'm surprised at you, seeing as how you're in the same position. I would have thought you would have more compassion."

Mrs. Munson was silent for a moment. "Maybe I'm not wonderful," she said softly. "If I were wonderful, how could he have done this to me?"

"Because he's a rat," said George with feeling. "Like me."

"You're not a rat."

"If I were your husband you'd think differently."

Adele Munson bit her lip and drank her coffee in silence.

"More coffee, Adele?"

"No, thank you, George. George, do I look old for my age?"

"What is your age?"

She sighed. "Being young is everything, these days. Isn't that why you ran after the girls? And I'll bet you're not sorry either, except that you were caught."

"The young can do things that we can't."

"Like what? Run the quarter mile in record time?" She sipped her coffee.

"Like time and freedom to do what they want."

"Well, none of that is going to rub off on you by shacking up with them."

"Divorce will do it," he stated flatly.

"So, go get a a divorce!"

"I thought you were on my side, Adele."

"Well, my side has rights too, plenty of them, and that time and freedom look pretty good to me, too."

They finished their coffee in silence.

"There's a movie about Chagall playing nearby. I hear it's very uplifting."

"And what will we do after it's over?"

"That's up to you, Adele."

"I mean to stay uplifted! Oh, you men!"

"Do you want me to run after young girls?"

"I don't care what you do!"

"I thought you did."

"Well, I don't."

There ensued another silence, in which Mrs. Munson, her arms folded across her chest, stared defiantly into space. George stared into his empty coffee cup.

"I'm out of coffee, Adele."

Involuntarily, she laughed. "What do you want me to do, brew you some?"

"I'm glad you said that. You could have said, 'Let's go.'"

"And I should have. Let's go, then, if you're finished."

"I'm not finished," he said aggressively, before lapsing into an awkward silence.

"Really, George," said Adele Munson rising, "this conversation is completely pointless."

"Tomorrow's will be better," he said, rising to help her on with her coat.

"No tomorrow," she said firmly. "You've got your problem and I've got mine. They are separate problems and are going to remain that way."

"Don't you feel that fate has thrown us together?"

"No, I don't. That's a lot of nonsense and you know it. No snow job in spring, please!" She pulled on her gloves.

"No need for gloves in spring either, Adele."

"And who made you an arbiter of fashion?"

He grinned. "Just trying to melt the snow."

She smiled.

★★★★★

Jane put the key into the lock and turned it to the right. She sighed. On the other side lay the comfortable duplex, unimaginable without Alan in it. But he would be home soon, home to their life together. For a split second a spasm of fear swept through her. She turned the knob and stared as the door swung open, then looked back at the hallway, the elevator, the domicile arrangements on the floor. They were the same as they had always been.

"But this is insane," she thought. "This is not my apartment!"

She stood amazed and undecided for a moment before she felt impelled to step inside and quietly close the door behind her.

"Is anyone here?" she asked clearly She could almost touch the stillness. "Some fine joke this is," she pronounced without relish. "I expect my furniture back and unscratched by tomorrow morning, do you hear? A pretty mess you've made of things." She looked disdainfully at her neat, orderly, strange surroundings. "I know you're here. Come out and face me this instant!"

She moved, somewhat dazed, through what had once been her living room and bedroom. They were awash with pastels, at the windows, on the sofa, on the chairs, pastels that looked familiar. On impulse, she opened the bedroom closet. It was empty. She looked again at the flounce on the bedspread, at the drapes a single cord could swing open and shut. They had been her favorite dresses. She sat down on the bed familiarly, though now disconcertingly, hard and gazed numbly through the bedroom door to the living room beyond. A woman swept into it, a woman all bronze and bouncy, who glared at her.

"Well, it's about time you're here." She tossed her blonde mane over her shoulder. "Get off my bed, please. Thank you. You're an hour late. Put on your uniform and get to work. My guests start arriving at nine o'clock."

"This is a dream, an insane dream!" thought Jane. "What am I supposed to do," she said aloud.

"Why everything! Weren't you told? I wanted a woman who can do everything: vacuum the upholstery, shampoo the rugs, polish the furniture, do the windows — I do hope you're one who does windows — polish the silverware, wash the dishes, cook a gourmet meal — good heavens, you'll have to go shopping; my cupboard is bare — serve the guests and make sure they mingle. The agency gave you my guest list. Have you checked the backgrounds, habits, food and chat likes and dislikes of those invited? How dreadful it would be if you said something out of the way. I'd be mortified!"

"Haven't you left out minding the children and storing the clothes?" suggested Jane.

"There are no children and there will be no clothes. My guests will arrive naked, so you need fear no distractions."

"Naked?" exclaimed Jane in wide-eyed wonder, and recoiled from her words with a sharp intake of breath. For she suddenly realized that she had said nothing, that the strange blonde woman had said nothing.

"Of course naked. But will you please put on your uniform and go about your business?"

"Like the rest of the furniture."

The woman smiled.. "Not quite. I can do without the furniture. I cannot do without you."

"I am indispensable?"

"You are important. I will return at eight-thirty. These preparations make me nervous."

The woman was gone before Jane could think of what to say. She wasn't sure whether the woman had walked out of the room or thought herself out of it.

"Penny!" Jane called out fiercely. Instead of the sound of her own voice she heard the growl of distant thunder. "What am I to do?" she whined plaintively. And the answer came to her: "Just as you were told."

In the living room she saw an overnight case she had not noticed before. Inside lay a blue and white linen uniform. She lifted it out, brushing it against the Lord & Taylor label on the case.

"The idea!" she exclaimed, as the image of her upcoming account bill flashed through her mind.

She searched for the vacuum cleaner.Where would Penny have kept it? She admitted ruefully that she didn't know where many of the appliances were kept in her own home. The ironing board, for instance. Not all the clothes she wore were polyester blends. They didn't all drip-dry; they weren't all innately free of care. In what secret place did Penny store the mechanism that smoothed out the furrows, that made everything all right. But she didn't need the iron. These people wee arriving naked. One by one she found the tools she needed. The vacuum cleaner in its cutaway coat stood solitary in the hall closet, the furniture wax seemed to cast a burnished glow of its own on the end table, and the silverware polish in its cut glass container seemed to conjure up the crystal and glitter of the party just hours away. By seven-thirty she had worked up a considerable sweat. She leaned back on her haunches to examine the leg of the table she had just polished and survey the room. It looked neat and clean, as it had when she first entered it, only now it really was. But it smelled like it, too. Was all this work really necessary? She fiddled with the knobs on the air conditioner and tried to find one that would cause the odors to be expelled from the apartment. But never having created such odors before, she was at a loss as to how to remove them.

"Penny, where are you?"

She opened every window in the house, reflecting that she did not have much time to prepare a meal. From somewhere in the air came a correction: "a gala dinner." Jane gave a determined nod as she marched through the hall and slammed the front door closed behind her.

The fresh air and familiar sights brought her to her senses, senses which told her that her artist's imagination had run away with her. Surely she needed no more than the help of a make-believe shrink like Dr. Schmeck. She wondered if he would see her again. But since she was on her way to the supermarket, why not continue? Why not cook that French epicurean delight she had prepared for Alan on their honeymoon night? She quickened her pace.

★★★★★

Jane found it difficult to see over the parcel pressed against her stomach. At the corner she stepped off the curb as the light turned green. A sudden screech of brakes and a monumental gust of wind threw her off balance and scattered the fruits of her shopping across the street. Two bystanders helped her to her feet.

"Are you'll right, lady?"

"Yes. Thank you so much," said Jane breathing heavily. "That car!" she exhaled.

"What car?" The man looked at the emptiness facing the traffic light. His eyes sighted up the street to the vehicles stopped for the light a block away.

Jane looked around, bewildered. "But I heard it screech to a stop, didn't you?"

"I don't hear these things anymore, lady. I tune them out. Your hearing's too sharp. The nearest car's a block away, so take it easy, relax, stop worrying."

"But that sudden wind!"

"Wind?" The man looked at his fellow Samaritan. "I'm afraid you're overheated, lady."

"But it's not hot."

He shook his head. "Believe me, lady, for you it's hot. I suggest you go into the restaurant right here and have a cup of tea. It'll sooth you."

The other man nodded, and as Jane gazed around, she saw a small knot of sympathetic faces nodding too. She accepted the groceries that had been collected for her and placed in the undamaged bag, thanked her helpers, and continued walking down the street, ignoring the restaurant and the cross street to her block. She couldn't go home, not now at least. Her thoughts were unfocused. She had to find a quiet place where no one would find her and where she could think. In the shadow of a building she saw an old woman with a cracked cigar box filled with change on the stoop beside her. Jane rested her shopping bag on the stoop. In response to the old woman's rattling of the box beneath her nose, she loosened her grip on the shopping bag and walked away.

She walked blankly, ignorant of the path her feet had chosen, thinking only of an unfelt wind, an unseen blonde, an unheard command, her bizarre and feverish activity at home, an apartment turned upside down — and Alan. She stopped and found herself facing a huge, imposing white building just off Fifth Avenue. It was her favorite mansion housing The Frick Collection. She forced her buckling knees to get her up the steps and to the sanctuary of the Court. The refreshing coolness and the sound of water soothed her mind, but as several people entered the area she retired to a bench on the edge of the East Colonnade. She sat there for a long time. Then she rose. Her feet found their way to the West Gallery. Vermeer's "Mistress and Maid" held her transfixed by the magic of light and color and an amorphous anxiety, while across the room a somber "Polish Rider" filled her with unreasonable fear. The Turners facing each other across the middle of the room bathed her senses in an outsized reality of mystical proportions. The portraits faded — the Rembrandt, the Hals, the Van Dyck — only the mood, the color of these others remained. Her eyes absorbed first one then the other. Her mind did not reason, but absorbed, until all blended inside her, until the rider and the harbors shared the mutuality of the mistress and maid, until the Turners crossed the room, frothing and splashing as they did so, until Jane found herself turning to warn the two women of the danger, until the two women turned upon her a questioning gaze. And Jane ran!

A clang of doors and the click of metal sounded unnaturally loud in her ears. She stopped abruptly, her eyes unaccountably turned toward the Oval Room. There, Diana the huntress, pedestaled and frozen in motion, suddenly continued her run, set arrow to bow, and took aim at Jane.

Chapter Five

JANE'S SHRIEK ECHOED INAUDIBLY, AND when she finally closed her mouth and stopped shaking, she stood mesmerized. Passing around her were ladies and gentlemen of every order. Their clothes looked substantial enough to touch if she dared, but of their bodies she saw nothing. This first shock led to another. Like gilded windows the frames encircled the rooms with views devoid of people where people had previously existed. The frames were empty. Fantastically accoutered bodies laughed and joked. At least accouterments without bodies looked fantastic, Jane thought. What purpose did they serve?

"A substantial assembly, don't you agree?"

Jane's eyes opened wide.

"I see you don't agree, but men and women are the substance of their clothes, are they not? Let me put you at ease, then. There, that's the best I can do."

Around the breathing in her ear evolved a young man, short, plump, in a tuxedo topped by a seemingly air-held mask.

"My features don't have the nobility of my clothes," he said, "but masks have always been a mortal rage. You had better cover your face. Here!" He circled a glove in the air and produced a fan.

Jane rallied "Her fan's the fairer face."

"That's the ticket!"

"My office window!" blurted Jane.

51

"These expressions will be my ruination. They're as tenacious as women, make it difficult to operate in other centuries and on other planes. Mother doesn't like them at all. The expressions, I mean, but at least they don't define me as they do Baron Kisaunof."

"Who are you?"

"Your companion for the evening. Call me Bunny. You realize, of course, that you've been naughty. You've run away from your assigned task. But that's as well, I suppose. It shows some spirit. And thanks to that spirit there have been a few changes and the party's had to be shifted here. The Frick is ours tonight. Isn't it grand? We're all delighted."

"Who — who are *we*?"

"Just look around and see. There's Lady Hamilton fingering Sir Thomas More's medallion. Mustn't touch, Lady Hamilton. Ah, and there's Madame Boucher talking to that young officer. His girlfriend isn't laughing now! Circumstances can certainly produce strange couplings. It makes existence interesting, don't you think? We've got a very democratic assembly. But we must make a proper entrance."

With that, they were whisked by an unseen hand to the doorstep of the mansion. A marionette in black tie and tails snapped to attention as he greeted them. He turned to face the interior and, addressing no one in particular, enunciated crisply, "Marquis de L'Amour et Mademoiselle," which echoed through every room in the mansion.

"It's madame," corrected Jane automatically.

"There is a little mademoiselle in every madame," said the Marquis, and the lips of his mask curved upward in a smile. "There's our hostess, Madame de Veneer. We must be presented."

They waited in a receiving line. Madame's mask gave serious attention to each guest for the space of ten seconds, then folded upward at the lips as it bobbed down in dismissal.

"Do as she does," whispered Bunny the Marquis, and Jane saw her predecessors on the line do likewise.

Madame's mask was milk white. She was encased in mint-green feathers mimicking her every movement. They heaved and subsided with her supposed breathing and seemed to have a life of their own. From her carefully curled, golden hair sprouted a large sprig of feathers that matched the color of her gown. Madame's glassy, silent glare chilled Jane, but she curved her false lips upward in the required smile.

"Oh, Bunny," she said, desperately wishing he had an arm she could clasp.

Bunny's mask nodded his sympathy, then turned its lips downward in despair.

Jane managed a smile. "Thank you, anyway."

The Marquis led her through the house, his thoughts silent. The eyes of Jane's mask were involuntarily wide with wonder. The women were elaborately bedecked with jewels suspended between masks and gown and hanging by their sides on invisible arms. Towering headdresses alternated with closely cropped heads, plumes with towers, ribbons with lace, and satins with silks. In the Court a baroque ensemble held sway, and in the Gallery a brass band, like a shiny magnet, drew a wardrobe accumulation of hundreds of years. In each of the other rooms a single musician strolled and played his silent music to the silent guests.

"Bunny, I want to leave."

"But we've only just arrived."

"I want to — please! I'm frightened."

"Of me?"

"Not of you. Somehow I feel comfortable with you, but these others, these fleshless, speechless zombies —"

"Zombies!" Bunny the Marquis seemed amused. "What's frightening about them?"

"Oh, don't be silly, Bunny. It's obvious! I mean it's *not* obvious. It's what I can't see that frightens me. It's what's going on under those masks."

"If you just squint your eyes and shut your mind, you'll find nothing unusual at all about these clotheshorses."

They passed before a huge wall-length mirror which seemed to enlarge the room and the number of its occupants and which presented Jane with a view of herself. She shrank back.

"Frightened of yourself, too?"

Jane gave him a wan smile. "I'm all right."

"Of course you are. You don't have to see your body to know you're here. Shall I introduce you to yourself, just to make sure?"

"You're being silly again." Jane laughed nervously and moved forward.

The Marquis watched her go.

She turned around suddenly.

"Yes, my dear. I wasn't sure you wanted me," he pouted.

Jane winced. "Don't do that. You look grotesque. Haven't you learned to control that mask by now?"

"You think flesh does a prettier job of it, I know, but your thoughts are the result of habit, not really thought at all. Anyway, I feel awkward wearing masks, but I did promise Mother. I'm supposed to behave, but oh, it would be so exciting to — Well, never mind. We'll have fun in spite of Mother. Dinner will be served at the stroke of nine. Until then, let's enjoy ourselves. Is there anybody you would like to meet?"

Jane looked around skeptically and shook her head.

"Good. Then I'll have you all to myself. I love to dance, do you?" And he led her onto the dance floor of the West Gallery.

Bunny guided Jane effortlessly over the floor.. She had no idea to what music they were dancing, but it didn't matter. With each whirl by her partner a fraction of fear dropped away, until no doubts or uncertainties remained. Then a carefree gaiety began to encircle the Gallery, and when the musicians no longer fingered their instruments, she still fancied she heard the music floating in the air. It mingled with an ethereal breeze that blew in from the lawn and spilled out again onto the portico along with some of the guests. It seemed natural to take Bunny's imagined arm and follow, but an usually bright-eyed mask blocked their way. Its lips were pursed.

"He begs an introduction," explained Bunny, "Baron Kiss, my charming protégé Madame Jane."

Jane raised an eyebrow. Baron Kiss raised both. His mask sprang into immediate and rapid motion in his apparent pleasure. Jane was at a loss for a response.

"Flattered bewilderment," whispered Bunny, "Excellent. You're doing well. The fool is in rare form. He loves a mystery. As who doesn't? Soon the bees will be buzzing his discovery throughout the mansion."

As though at a given signal, a hissing sound stirred faintly from the portico doors and swelled to an unseemly degree, unseemly even if the mansion had been alive with sound, which it was not.

"Crude," said Jane, and Bunny felt rightfully abashed, but not the least bit sorry.

"Oh, Bunny! What will these people think of a madame formally announced as a mademoiselle?"

Bunny made no response, but the eyes set into his mask sparkled with the brilliance of one whose contact lenses had caught the light.

Bunny swept her out onto the portico steps as a young gallant would. Then he stopped and looked at the lawn with misgivings. Jane read his thoughts with ease.

"Madame de Veneer has almost left us in the dark," she said, eying the thin slice of moon, "but we have some bright and beautiful stars."

"Not stars," said Bunny darkly, "planets."

"Can you make out which ones?"

"Of course," flashed Bunny, somewhat offended. "Venus, Uranus, and Neptune. Drat it! Why didn't she have Jupiter?"

"But these are lovely," soothed Jane.

Bunny kicked a pebble. "I wanted Jupiter. She knew I wanted Jupiter."

"Well," said Jane with a shrug of her dress and a sparkle of her jeweled eyes, "shall we explore the garden?"

"You may, if you wish," he said, sitting himself on the top stair, "but I won't budge." He hurled a petulant look at the planets clustered above. "I wanted Jupiter."

"But you can't just sit here," said Jane, dismayed. "I need you! You can't abandon me now!"

"Believe me, you're not abandoned," said Bunny, his mask hanging down his shirt. "I'm the one who's been abandoned. She always treats me like a child."

"Madame de Veneer?" asked Jane, somewhat bewildered.

"No, Mother."

Jane sat down beside him. "Someone's always telling us what to do, controlling our lives." She sighed.

Bunny's drooping mask lifted a little. "Oh, it's not all that bad for you. You can walk into the West Gallery and scream your head off or march right out the door. You have limited choices, but choices nonetheless."

"But how can I possibly guess where each of these choices will lead me?"

"Great Jupiter! Why would you want to know that?"

"I like to know where I'm going, whenever possible. Not that I don't like pleasant surprises. They're all right. I just want to avoid the other kind. It's common sense."

Bunny looked astounded. "Even Mother makes mistakes! Didn't anyone ever tell you you don't learn from your successes, that you've got to make mistakes, that sometimes it's even fun?"

"That's why I'm here, isn't it. Well, it's no fun."

A faint sound of music verging on the subsonic wafted out into the garden.

"You've got the wrong attitude," said Bunny.

"You and I both," retorted Jane.

Bunny stood and seemed to lift her to her feet "I needed that."

"Why did — why did she choose me?"

"You're a Taurus. Mother rules your sign. And this is your sixth anniversary year and your thirty-sixth year on earth, the number six and a multiple of six.'

"And six is the number of Venus," said Jane softly.

Bunny's mask bobbed agreement. "And Mother loves the spring. She won't be pleased to hear me talking business. Come on, let's have some fun fast." He giggled, turned, and walked into a wall.

"Bunny!" shouted Jane, as he crumpled onto the top step-and-a-half.

"Bunny?" came a voice from behind her.

"Help me get him up! Or a doctor. Is there a doctor in the house?"

"May I see the child?"

Jane turned at the gentle voice behind her. It belonged to a brown-robed, ascetic-looking man with a fringe of hair around the rim of a bald head.

"I'm a doctor of sorts," he explained kindly.

Jane moved aside. She could see and hear him! The man leaned over Bunny.

Bunny shook his head and moaned. Jane and the stranger got him to his feet. He swayed and they steadied him, helping him to a sitting position on the top step.

"Was there a call for a doctor?" A man with a long, white beard set in a stern face towered over them in a scarlet robe.

"Oh, Jerome," said the stranger pleasantly, "it's all right. The bunny will live." His eyes twinkled.

"Are you saying an animal is injured, Francis?"

"Merely a two-legged bunny, Jerome. You *are* all right, child?"

"Yes, yes, I'm all right," said Bunny, looking in amazement from Francis to Jerome. "You're not about to frighten me."

Jerome gave him a thunderous look, but Francis said kindly, "Now, now, we mean you no harm. You are a foolish boy, but then," he sighed, "it runs in your family. We did not ask to be invited here, you know."

Bunny's brow creased, and Jane realized that his features, like his saviors' were also now clearly visible. His mask was gone.

"My fault," he admitted. "This house was my idea. I thought I'd sent all party poopers elsewhere for the duration."

Francis shrugged. "Well," he said, "it's good to be reminded of what it was like, of what it is still like down her. Where we are we tend to forget the panorama of life on earth, working as we do only on those appeals sincere enough and strong enough to reach us."

"I beg to differ with you, Francis," boomed Jerome. "The smear of the world is indelibly etched on my memory. You," he said, turning to Bunny "have been responsible for damaging the hearts and minds of untold millions. You have misdirected piety away from its proper source and into false channels leading to unhappiness and hell. You are the cause of much misery in the world and we two," he said, linking an arm through Francis', "we two, in this house of iniquity meet you on your own grounds, will do battle with you on your own soil, and will win, so will it heaven above!"

"Jerome," whispered Francis, "we are trespassing on private property. We have as little right here as they. Perhaps we should concentrate on restoring to the Frick what belongs to it by law, and all of us depart the scene."

"The law of God supersedes the law of gods," boomed Jerome. "This opportunity to save lost souls must not be abandoned. The sphere in which we find them, unless it be hell, whither of course we never go, is no obstacle to the saving grace. You know that, Francis," he admonished gently.

"Oh, what a night of it we shall have," sighed Francis.

"The work of the Lord is no burden, and a night is as a lifetime, time enough for the task set before us."

"Perhaps, dear Jerome, we might reset our task and start, and possibly end, with this young lady. Her position is still quite elementary. Mortality still courses through her body."

Jerome beamed at Francis. "And so it does. Burdened with care and caught in the pagan snare," he said darkly.

"She's mine!" shouted Bunny. "You can't have her. Get away from us this instant or I'll move the party someplace else!"

Jerome looked overhead. The moon had almost completely disappeared behind some sudden clouds, leaving the garden in shadowy light. Jerome looked triumphantly at Bunny.

"You didn't do that, so don't look so smug. Mother is allowing me to stand on my own feet, that's all, and I can!" He got up shakily. "Mother's worth ten of you!"

"And how many of me do you think *you* are worth?"

Bunny grabbed Jane roughly by the arm. "Come on, we've got a party to enjoy."

"Young lady," said Jerome, lightly laying both hands on hers "you believe in God, do you not? Would you rather not find your way with us?"

Jane faltered. "I — I appreciate your offer, but — but I'm with someone already." And she turned away with Bunny into the crowded hall.

"Nice to hear a young man speak well of his mother," said Francis pleasantly, looking up at the sky, "regardless."

★★★★★

Ann did not love him, at least not enough to marry him, and he wanted to marry her. Don Bryon strode moodily down Fifth Avenue, his hands in his pockets. The rain had stopped, but the sky was still overcast, and the trees in Central Park looked woebegone and inconsolable. It just didn't make sense, but there it was. He had never proposed marriage to anyone else, no, not to one of his bookful of beauties. She wasn't as beautiful as some or as brainy as others, but she was the only one he cared about. Why couldn't she feel the same way about him? He was tall, dark-haired, and handsome, a Prince Charming if ever he'd seen one, and he was rich and generous. What more could a woman want? Perhaps he had offered her too much, and yet she had been gladly accepting. But it was her nature not to believe in dreams come true. They are fairy tales, so she refused to let them come to pass. The logical conclusion of a dream had to be a disappointment, so she saw to it that it was. What was he to do? He would shower her with gifts. How could she refuse him then? But one each day, each twenty-four hour day would not be enough. He would send one each hour, one each minute. She would be overwhelmed, he thought happily — and throw it and him over, he concluded gloomily. Ann was different. She required something different. "I just can't think what," he murmured. He stopped to watch the aimless pigeons on the steps of St. Patrick's Cathedral. Then he heavily climbed to the entrance.

His entrance marked the exit of a dark-haired, middle-aged woman fidgeting with the gloves in her hands. Adele Munson stood uncertainly looking down Fifth Avenue. She saw a slouch-brimmed hat in a doorway across the street. The face of the wearer wasn't visible, but she was irritated all the same.

"Oh, why doesn't he leave me alone! Everywhere I go, on every street, in every store!" A couple turned to stare at her. She quickly walked down the steps and crossed the street. "George, you're going to leave me alone! I will not have any more of this, do you hear?"

"I love you, Adele."

"Shush, you fool!" she said, looking hastily around. "You don't even know me. We're almost total strangers. Go home to your wife and children."

"The kids are married. The wife doesn't want me."

"Well, I don't want you either. Go follow some other woman. There must be some woman who would want you."

"You're the only woman I want, Adele. Give me a chance."

"Why must you torment me like this? Why? Why? I've got a good mind to fire Gilbey, go home, and suffer with that beast I'm chained to by holy writ. You're driving me to it, George!" she said, wringing her gloves.

"You're too good for me, Adele. You're too good for me."

"Oh, Lord, not that line again. I won't hear another word. I'm warning you. Leave me alone or I'll have you arrested for harassment!" She strode off angrily.

George looked forlornly after her. A minute later he ascended the Cathedral steps.

★★★★★

With a slight toss of his head Jerome beckoned Francis to follow him. Bundling him into a corner he hissed, "They've got a plan."

"Most likely," replied Francis. "Can you guess at its substance?"

"Love, Francis. It will be love," sneered the tall man. "And a lot they know about it!"

"The young lady wears a marriage band," said Francis thoughtfully, ignoring his companion's tone.

"They're using their wiles to persuade her to break her marriage vows."

"Or to avoid their dissolution."

"That sham goddess and her offspring? Don't make me laugh!"

Francis refrained from saying he did not think that possible. "We should determine the facts before we intervene, the facts and the spirit into which the adventure has been entered."

"The facts, most decidedly. It's easy to imagine the spirit of the adventure."

Francis half-checked himself, then laughed. "We never did see eye to eye in the Living Hall. You always seemed bigger than life, fixing me with an intense stare from across the room, while I, small in relation to my surroundings, sent my prayers and my gaze to heaven."

"That was most unkind, Francis, and unworthy of you."

"Now, now, Jerome, take no offense. It is not you and I who are framed for examination, merely our images. Even now, it is only our images that speak through these painted forms, a tribute to the artistic geniuses who could bring us to the threshold of life."

"And the powers of evil who brought us over that threshold."

"But we are as we are. I feel no inappropriate urges, no stirrings of — no! No stirrings of lust at all," Francis said with decision.

Jerome's eyes widened in his solemn face.

"Only joking, Jerome, only joking."

"If I cannot take you seriously, we will not be able to act together in Christian charity and for the love of God to save this young woman."

"We must allow for the possibility that she may not need saving."

"Can you doubt it?" Jerome was astonished. "But even if these devil's disciples have a noble purpose, victory must lie with God," he thundered.

"Hush," urged Francis. "It will, anyway."

"Facts," whispered Jerome. "We must get them, stick to them, and act upon them. Most of the guests can know nothing. They are merely painted images, representatives of their real selves come to life. I know what you are about to say. Don't interrupt me with your thoughts. God's saints are exceptions. Their very shadows breathe knowledge and power. Now don't bring that up again. Where was I? Oh, yes. Madame de Veneer and Baron Kisonauf should be our starting points. Chances of getting information from that belligerent Bunny or his elusive mother, who is quite literally hanging around, are nil, I'm afraid. But what we are is obvious. No information will be forthcoming to us in our present forms. We must disguise ourselves. Yes, yes, I know we are not really we, but we must disguise even our seeming presences. What do you say, Francis?"

"It seems that I've said quite a lot already, but additionally I feel impelled to say that I agree."

"Well spoken, Francis There may be some difficulty in obtaining disguises from two of the guests. They may require some persuasion to part with them and assume ours. If not, there is surely a closet in which to conveniently store these people until we are done."

It was now Francis' turn to be surprised. "Well!" he exhaled. "And whom have you chosen to be?"

"General John Burgoyne, The Reynolds' portrait in the Dining Room. God's general. Suitable. What form will you assume?"

"I don't know! I'd rather remain myself, if you don't mind. Such complications are more your sphere than mine."

"Nonsense. You underrate your ability. You needn't select a general or an aristocrat. What about Titian's young man or Rembrandt's self portrait?"

"They're not like me at all."

"Not like you! They're not supposed to be like you. You're supposed to be like them, one of them! Don't be a prima donna, Francis. This will just be a temporary acting assignment in the service of the Lord. We have no time to waste. Whom will you be?"

"I have no idea. How do you plan to persuade the general to part with his identity for the evening?"

"Well, I thought I would give the man a fair chance. I will take him upstairs for a private chat and try to get his voluntary compliance with our plan."

"*Your* plan."

"If he refuses, I will use mild physical force to subdue him, gag him, and tie him to the bedpost, or perhaps I'll roll him under the bed, all in the spirit of the Crusades."

"Better to put him to bed with a companion. Force would be unnecessary."

"Are you with me or are you not?" asked the tall saint coldly.

Francis clapped him on the shoulder. "I'm with you."

★★★★★

"You waltz beautifully."

Jane circled the room gracefully on Bunny's arm. Her eyes sparkled.

Bunny grasped her more tightly around the waist and whirled her with dizzying speed across the floor.

"Bunny!" she half gasped, half laughed.

"Must - make - the - most - of - it," her pudgy companion puffed. "The minuet's next."

"Pardon me."

They continued to whirl. Jane turned her head too late to see the speaker.

"Pardon me."

Bunny whirled Jane more ferociously. "He's nobody," he said in answer to her look.

"Pardon me."

"Persistent beast. Let him find someone else."

"Who?"

"Baron Kiss."

"Pardon me," chimed a duo. And suddenly Bunny was whirling around with Lady Hamilton and Jane was in the arms of a tall, dark-haired man with the most luminous eyes she had ever seen.

"I beg your pardon mademoiselle, but I've been watching you all evening and have been so anxious to be with you again."

"But have we been introduced?"

"I've had the pleasure. Ah, the pleasure, the pleasure!" He rolled his eyeballs upward and drew her closer. "I am Baron Kisonauf. Monsieur le Marquis, in a friendly spirit of competition, has dubbed me Baron Kiss."

"I hate to disillusion you, Baron, but I don't think the spirit is all that friendly."

"Dear beautiful lady, I likewise hate to disillusion you, but look."

Jane looked toward the doors framing the portico in time to see Bunny descend the steps, both hands clasping those of Lady Hamilton.

"A most appealing lady. The talk of the town in her day. No reflection on you, my dear. I doubt that you have had either the opportunity or the inclination to do likewise."

"Alan, Alan Blaiser," she thought irrationally. "I — I'd like to sit down," she said falteringly.

"But of course. Forgive me. I am inconsiderate as well as tactless tonight." He led her to one of the chairs lining the walls and eased her into it. "I am not always this way, but you are a new experience for me, a beautiful new experience."

"I? How do you mean?"

"You are a creator, I've been told. That painted beauty on the arm of Monsieur le Marquis could have been your doing had Romney not thought of her first. That voluptuous Madame Boucher could have been your doing."

"You've omitted the delightful Bruni and that distinguished Jodrell," teased Jane.

"Those too. You could well have created me. You may, yet."

"Baron Kis — Kisonauf, you would not want to look like one of my paintings. Anyway, I've retired from creating. Now I display the creations of others in an art gallery."

"But you still have the power. You have not lost the power."

Jane felt uneasy. She looked toward the portico doors. "I would rather not talk about business, if you don't mind."

"My apologies. Of course not. The night was made for love. You do not find me irresistible?"

Jane frowned and lifted her lower lip. "I'm afraid not, though for a moment — " She laughed nervously. "You have possibilities."

"Shall we start again? A more formal beginning, mademoiselle."

"Baron Kisonauf, I am not a mademoiselle."

"Please! Say no more! I have complications enough in my life. Where ignorance is bliss 'tis folly to be wise."

The strains of a minuet began to fill the room.

"Will you do me the honor?"

"Oh, but I don't know how! All those steps …"

65

Baron Kiss took her arm. "There are some things a woman is born knowing. Sometimes, temporarily, she just forgets." And he led her to the center of the room.

Jane found the minuet relaxing, despite the need for partial concentration on what her feet were doing. The slow tempo slowed down life, and made the headlong rush toward the unknown acceptable, if not comprehensible. The minuet set up a structure to lean against. It was a comfort. The glow emanating from the Baron's eyes cast a reflection in hers. He knew it and looked away when she faced him directly, but when her eyes were on her feet or on the other guests matching the elegance and composure of the dance with their own, she felt a flush of warmth bathe her left cheek or the top of her head, or wherever the gaze of Baron Kisonauf had alighted. Bunny was reveling in the company of a Lady Hamilton. Was Alan doing the same? Was he enjoying himself as little as she? Here she was, taken in hand by Venus, made a part of an entertainment that gave her no joy and could instruct her in no way. She had mismatched herself with a darling man as impractical as he was affectionate. No night of magic and adventure could change that, could change her or Alan. The Baron broke into her thoughts with his own.

"'The eyes are the windows of the soul.' What nonsense! They are no more me than are my lips, my hands, my voice. My eyes dazzle, attract, repel. One, two, three, and I am on the sidewalk in my fancy clothes, a victim of appearances." He did not look at Jane as he spoke, but seemed, rather, to be addressing his toes.

Jane, surprised and somewhat ruffled by this introspective sally, made no response, and the minuet continued on its orderly, predictable way.

The dance over, the Baron led her to a smorgasbord in the Enamel Room. He took a delicately patterned piece of china from the sideboard.

"What would you like, my dear?" he asked simply.

Jane's eyes opened a bit wider, and she looked up into his. The erotic Baron, the aggressive Baron, the introspective Baton, and now the modest, self-effacing Baron. Even in the fully lit room his eyes shone. She felt very sorry for him.

"Perhaps a sampling?" he suggested. "Bite-size delights to whet your appetite for the magnificent dinner to follow." He heaped her plate.

"Aren't you eating, Baron?"

"You are feast enough for my eyes. I cannot attend to your needs if I am busy with my own."

He led her to a chair and bowed her into it before placing her plate on a mini table a few feet away and moving it in front of her.

"You are very kind," she said, "but needlessly so. In my day women are self-sufficient. We are used to doing things for ourselves. In fact we prefer to."

"Dear lady, women have always been self-sufficient, but I am sorry I have offended you."

"Oh, no, Baron! Forgive me. It is I who have been offensive."

He took her hands in his. "You could never offend, never."

"Believe me, Baron, I can." She was close to tears.

The Baron moved the food-filled table to a side. "Never!" he repeated, falling to his knees, clasping her hands more firmly in his, and burying her head in his lap. "Never me, never anyone who loves you!"

Jane touched his hair and shook her head at the blurry room.

"You do not believe that I love you?"

Jane sighed. "How would a woman of your time say it?"

"That she questions the sincerity of such a sudden devotion."

"Yes. Love at first sight is for fairy tales, and not for this one."

"Perhaps I overstated my case," he admitted, getting to his feet.

Jane shot a broad smile up at his face. "You're a nice man, Baron Kisonauf. I like you."

"Thank you. I want you to know that the fervor of my emotion was real. In some future time or place it could very well be love.

Right now it is need. I need you Mademoiselle Jane. I need you to make all my future manifestations, all my future lives and loves worth dreaming of. Look at me. You see! You dare not look me in the eyes. They blind you, not with love, but with pity, not with pleasure, but with pain. It was not always so. I misused my looks, my manners. My appetite was insatiable; that is why I care so little for food now. Look to what depths it has sunk me. Baron Kiss, the mocked and mimicked Baron Kiss, whose lusts so devoured him they coalesced in his eyes, making the sight of him unbearable and putting an end to his notorious escapades, his happiness, and his life."

"You committed suicide?"

"As the natural outcome of my behavior. The light from my eyes reflected in a roadside pond so blinded me for an instant, that I stepped onto the road and into the path of a coach and four."

"And there was no cure."

"There was no cure," echoed the Baron. "And no hope of one until now."

"My dear Baron, don't look at me that way. I would help you if I could, but I am powerless to solve my own problem, let alone yours."

"But a greater power than yours thinks otherwise. With a little guidance your story will have a happy ending. That is why you were invited here, was it not? I was not invited. I crashed, my need was so great. Monsieur le Marquis made an allowance for me to stay, but he can do no more. You are the chosen of Venus. If you choose me, perhaps I will be granted a cure and another chance. I am yours to command if you will do a deed of kindness that will set your seal on eternity!"

Jane shook her head. "Not that I don't want to, I simply can't. Why not ask the Goddess herself?"

"She won't help me."

"How do you know if you don't ask?"

"She won't help me," he repeated. "You're my only hope."

"There is a reason she won't help you, isn't there?"

The Baron heaved a monumental sigh. "I trifled with the affections of one of her protégés. She said, 'You want every woman you see, which is clearly more than you deserve. From this day forth this rapacious desire shall be clearly visible to everyone. You shall be Baron Kisonauf of the bright eyes, of the devouring eyes; Baron Kisonauf of the voracious appetite, Baron Kisonauf the glutton.' And so it has been."

"But you are dead! I cannot believe that Venus would hold a grudge beyond the grave."

"First of all, I am not dead, as you put it," he said with some asperity. "My aliveness to you may appear transitory, but I assure you, in the sphere in which I now move my peers consider me quite alive. In the second place, please refer to my answer in the first place. The Goddess has made no attempt to approach me, and all my attempts to approach her have been rebuffed."

"Still, if she allowed you to attend tonight when you so obviously don't belong …"

"Yes, she makes sure everything I do is obvious."

"… then perhaps she is giving you a chance to work your way out of her bad graces and her punishment."

"Please, please!" He gazed around with trepidation. "The Goddess of Love has no bad graces. I who worshipped her not wisely but too well know that. But as you say, there is a chance, a chance for me through you."

"You know," Jane said thoughtfully, "perhaps you were meant to meet two other uninvited guests, Saint Francis and Saint Jerome. Bunny, I mean the Marquis, meant to exclude them from the party, but they're here."

"Perish the thought! Render unto Caesar what is Caesar's, not Venus'. It is blasphemy to even think they … and yet they are here, as you say. A tangled web is being woven," he said ominously, "and I - we - must take care not to catch our feet in it."

"The plot thickens."

"Indeed it does. We must throw ourselves, with dignity of course, on the mercy of Madame de Veneer. She may know all. Look at her, gracious in multicolor splendor, holding high conclave with Lady Peel and the Duque de Osuna. Stay close to me and act natural."

He steered her through the ballroom to Madame de Veneer's side. They hovered briefly on the periphery of the trio before their hostess, extending her hands to them, brought them into the group and the conversation.

"Baron Kisonauf, you know the Duke, I believe?"

"We met once. I am glad of this opportunity to meet you again."

"Opportunity," grumbled the Duke. "He knows my wife. Very well."

"And how is the Duchess these days?"

"As usual," sighed the Duke with resignation.

"And Lady Peel, the astonishing Lady Peel," said Madame de Veneer, "meet Baron Kisonauf."

"Lady Peel, this is an honor." The Baron bowed deeply.

"So you've dusted off 'honor' for this occasion," said Madame with a broad smile.

"When the shoe fits —"

"You put it in your mouth," finished his hostess.

"You have forgotten the truism of 'ladies first.' Yes, Madame, even at the end of the twentieth century!" said the Baron.

"And certainly we are in the company of ladies," she responded subdued. "Lady Peel, this is Mademoiselle Jane Blaiser, an artist of the twentieth century. I assume you know what Baron Kisonauf is."

"Mademoiselle, Baron how do you do," Lady Peel said warmly. "Am I to understand that you two are the odd couple?"

Baron Kisonauf cleared his throat. "Madame de Veneer judges my present by my past, an understandable and forgivable error. But I stand before you ladies, and before you Duke, as a gentleman, a solid citizen of our dimension, a new man, as one would say. Witness my lovely lady companion. There is much truth to judging people by the company they keep."

"Hmph," grunted the Duke.

"Men of your sort, Baron, always talk too much," said Madame de Veneer. "Ladies, though they be ladies, still have tongues, I think."

"Ma - dame de Veneer," rasped Jane.

"Well, perhaps not," said the hostess.

Lady Peel laughed. "Cynthia, for shame! Jane Blaiser, I am Julia Peel of the domestic scene, patron of eight, and I hope you won't bypass me for Don Pedro, patron of the arts."

"I beg your pardon, Julia, but your knowledge of the arts is hardly to be taken lightly, and neither are my contributions to the domestic scene, all four of them."

Lady Peel laughed again. "Very well, Duke." She turned to Jane. "It's been so long since I've met someone of the first dimension, that I hope you won't mind our sharing you for a while. Would you mind, Baron?"

"Well, yes. I thrive in her company."

"Possessive, possessive," clucked Madame de Veneer."

"But if you don't take her too far, that is, if you will remain in this room ..."

"Just over there." Lady Peel pointed to a settee.

"Yes, well — certainly."

"Tired of her already?" murmured Madame de Veneer, as she brushed by the Baron.

Her feathers tickled his nose and he sneezed. "Reputation, reputation," he muttered, miserably. Wiping his nose in his handkerchief, he hurried after his hostess.

"Madame, you do me a terrible injustice."

She kept walking. "Lady Innes, how lovely you look."

"I tell you Madame, you do me a disservice."

She kept walking. "Pietro Aretino, you old devil, are you having a good time?"

"You've hurt my feelings needlessly," pursued the Baron.

71

She stopped and faced the Baron. "Whatever are you talking about? Leopards and tigers do not grow docile, and Baron Kisonaufs do not grow honest. You are what you are, and there's an end to it." She turned to go.

"No! You are wrong and I can prove it to you."

"You can't, you know you can't, and why should you? Enjoy what you are. *We* do."

"Madame —"

"Baron, I have *invited* guests to attend to. You *do* understand."

And she left him. He heard her shrill-voiced artificial amenities spread thinly around the room. This one was witty, that one was his usual charming self. He felt wretched. Was that the point? Was the Goddess suffering a fool gladly, in the magnanimity of her revenge? Well, at least he was not fodder for further foolery; he was being thoroughly ignored. No sooner had he thought this than a thin-fingered tap on his right shoulder caused him to turn around.

"I have been watching you," said handsome General Burgoyne. "There is a light in your eyes."

"Don't I know it," mourned the Baron. "My sins shine from them."

"Sins are evil, my friend. Evil does not manifest itself in light. God does."

For the first time that evening the Baron's distress gave way to fright. He had no intention of cozying up to this stranger — the General had in the past considered him beneath notice — and he was horrified at the possibility that the light in his eyes might be interpreted as saintliness rather than evil. Public opinion, he had found, always made it difficult to overcome appearances. When your evil was well-spoken of, opportunities to atone for it were always sparse.

"I am afraid your virtues do not make you welcome company, Baron, but I have taken the liberty of speaking to you on just that account. I have much to learn from you."

"You mistake me, General. I am a poor sinner."

"Spoken like a man of God! But what brings you here? You are all but a man of the cloth, and those, so I've been told, have been banished from this house for the night. Are you on a soul-saving mission?"

"I must insist you are mistaken in me, and the only soul I am intent on saving is my own."

"Ah, then the light is one of intent rather than of achievement. Still, most commendable. We are brothers in our search."

"I don't think so." He eyed Jane, deep in conversation with Lady Peel.

"Your looks belie your words. Surely you do not mean that you turn your back on light, on love, on Venus?"

"Venus? I am all ears."

"Venus, of course. My dear man, do you not know that Venus is a messenger of God?"

The Baron's mouth fell open. "No!" he ejaculated.

"Oh, yes indeed!"

"You mean like an angel?"

"Just so."

"I'm as innocent as a babe in the woods. Why was I never told? But wait, that cannot be. Venus is angry with me. She would not give me this lovelight, even if she is an angel. Anyway, Venus herself told me this light is punishment."

"Oh, there is no question that it was. But the punishment of the angel has been transformed by the grace of God. The glare of evil has been transformed into the light of good. Do not tell me that you have not noticed the difference."

"No, I haven't."

"But you must. Look in this mirror."

"The Baron looked. "Now that you mention it, there is a softness around the monumental shine…."

"Like a halo."

"But the brassy brightness …"

"Gold, man! Have you never seen the stuff? A guardian angel is on your side now. Naturally Venus had a reason for this party tonight, one to which you are no doubt privy."

The Baron was silent.

"You needn't tell me, of course, since I already know."

"I'm relieved to hear it," said the Baron. "Could you begin our friendship by getting Mademoiselle Jane away from Lady Peel? I'd like to talk to her."

"With pleasure."

"Pleasure," muttered the Baron, as he watched the General, his military bearing loudly proclaiming his presence, stride confidently toward the ladies. "One man's pleasure takes another man's measure. Words, words."

Jane hurried to the Baron's side. "Lady Peel has detained the General. He said he would rejoin us momentarily."

"Oh," groaned the Baron. "She's testing my loyalty; she's using the General as decoy. What a story! He must think I was born yesterday."

"Who is she? What story?"

"She - her - oh, you know — the Goddess! That nincompoop general tried to convince me that she — oh, Venus! — worked for God. As an angel, mind you! But believe me, she's self-employed. She takes orders from no one. I won't betray her; I won't be tricked into doing it, either. But Madame de Veneer and General Burgoyne are strange bedfellows. Cruelty and kindness. More Janus than Venus. Very strange. Come with me."

The Baron all but pulled her through the Gallery, the Oval Room, and the Court to the majestic staircase leading to the second floor. Jane, with considerable effort, wrenched her hand free from his and, breathing heavily, stood her ground.

"You can't keep running, at least you can't keep running with me."

For a moment Baron Kisonauf stared at her in disbelief, then his shoulders sagged, and as his eyes involuntarily blazed, his face folded into dozens of valleys, his nose and cheek bones protruding like sharp projections revealed on the ocean floor when the tide is sucked away from them.

Jane was instantly sorry. She joined him on the stairs, and together they sat and stared down the South Hall.

Leaning over the railing on the first landing watching the two was a young woman in a blue satin dress. She had a red ribbon in her hair and a faint Mona Lisa smile on her smooth, round face. She tapped on the railing with a stick.

The two turned around.

She smiled.

The Baron stood up, his still cadaverous face registering uncertainty. Jane stood up too, and without hesitation joined the woman on the landing. From up close the woman looked even younger and more innocent, but her smile seemed less Mona than mischief.

"I'm Jane Blaiser, Comtesse. You're one of my favorites at the Frick."

"It's kind of you to say so, but I do believe you mean it!"

"She doesn't say so to all the paintings, believe me," said the Baron, now at their side.

The Comtesse d' Haussonville smiled again. "You must excuse my voice. Frick patrons have coughed on me rather unmercifully this past week."

"My, my," said the sympathetic Baron "Oh my, yes! You must attend to that throat. Such hoarseness is not to be sneezed at."

"I should hope not!" The Comtesse's eyes opened wide. "I've been caressing my throat with wine. Have you ever tried it?"

"I never thought of caressing quite in that place," said the Baron.

"You must try it some time."

"Anything you say, Comtesse." He bowed.

"You know, Baron, some day your passion for trite expressions and borrowed wisdom will get you into trouble. What if I actually asked you to do whatever I said?"

"I would do it. I am a man of integrity; I stick by what I say."

"Very well, then. I am asking you to remove the wig worn by Madame de Veneer."

For a moment Baron Kisonauf stood quite still. "You're joking, of course."

"I am not."

"But why?"

"I owe you no explanation; you said you would do as I say."

"She is my hostess, against whose murder I should shut the door, not bear the knife myself."

"She embarrassed you before two very respectable guests and uncovered what you are. Why should you not uncover what she is?"

"And she was wrong, dead wrong. She's an unforgiving, painted old lady, but two wrongs don't make a right."

"True, but they don't necessarily make a wrong, either."

"Jane, what do you think?"

"What does it matter what I think. Life rolls on in whatever dimension – first, second – regardless of what we think. Things seem to happen regardless of what we do or don't do."

"But what things? You've painted yourself into a corner, Mademoiselle, as I have in the past. At least I'm trying to paint myself out of it."

"With what success?"

"You certainly know how to hurt a guy."

"The truth hurts."

"Only for a little while," said the Comtesse. "But really, you two are beginning to sound alike. I do believe you are a team!"

"Similar expressions," admitted Jane grudgingly, "but different sentiments."

"That doesn't matter. As long as you have something in common, however small, you can be a team of sorts even across the dimensions."

She looked Jane in the eyes. "What do you say?"

The Baron took her arm. "For better, for worse?"

Jane took a deep breath. "Well, why not!"

The Comtesse d'Haussonville watched them march off with the sudden exuberance of decision. She did not follow. She leaned against the banister, her hand on her chin, then descended the stairs and walked to the front door. The hall was empty. The marionette in black tails was gone, and as she closed the door behind her, the Comtesse was, too.

Chapter Six

"WE NEED A PLAN, BARON, a plan that will allow you to keep your word without opening you to the ridicule of everyone here. There's no reason for anyone to know who is responsible for Madame de Veneer's unwigging."

"True, my dear Jane. The Comtesse didn't say I had to make a fool of myself. Let's dance toward Madame. I'd like a better look at that wig."

Madame de Veneer was in rapt conversation with The Polish Rider. General Burgoyne was at her side. They looked a ridiculous trio. It was more than the incongruity of apparel which first struck the eyes. It was an aura of certainty, veiled, a matter-of-fact acceptance of himself that emanated from the Rider. He was at ease in his faded, dusty clothes talking to the old, painted Madame and the stiff, decorated General. He looked the most ethereal and insubstantial figure in the room, yet, somehow, the most real.

The Baron eyed the feathers. "You slip," he whispered into Jane's ear, "and I clutch the nearest thing in an attempt to keep from falling — those feathers. I fall, hopefully without breaking any bones, perhaps on top of Madame de Veneer, a soft cushion, and her wig goes flying."

"You might hurt her. You wouldn't want to do that."

The Baron grimaced.

"Venus wouldn't like it," warned Jane.

"I shouldn't have promised."

"But you did. What about the lights? A short circuit, perhaps?"

"I'm not an electrician."

"How about a bandit? With a mask on and a change of clothes you could pluck her wig, escape through the garden, change behind a bush, and return, all innocence, to the party."

The Baron danced her away from their prey. "Yes," he said solemnly, "a change of identity, to honor the Comtesse's request and to escape the vengeance of Venus. I must have a change of identity. It is the only way. With Uranus and Saturn above, it was meant to be. It is written overhead this night."

"And you will succeed!"

"But Venus, Venus ..." he muttered disconsolately. "Perhaps Mars will intercede in my behalf. Come. We will walk slowly toward the hall, smiling, smiling courteously at everyone; that's right. Then we will look cautiously about to make sure the coast is clear and make a mad dash up the stairs. There you will make me a new man while the spell is on, and we shall hope for the best."

Jane eyed him with wonder, then hurried after him. At the top of the landing he put his fingers to his lips and tiptoed to the nearest door. It was locked. He stole quietly toward the next one and turned the knob.

The curtains were drawn, but the light streaming in from the hall revealed it to be a study. The Baron walked toward the desk and opened all the drawers.

"You have what you need here. And here" he said, pulling away a white brocade coverlet, inexplicably resting on the sofa.

"Need for what?"

"You said you would help me, for better for worse, remember?" Something more than light shone from his eyes. "You are an artist. Tonight Venus has brought the paintings in this house to life. Any painted human image in this mansion cannot escape the illusion of life in the first dimension. I am asking you to paint my image, my false image. I will drape this brocade over myself, just so, and you will paint my outline with new features, which I leave to your creative instincts."

Jane looked at him aghast. "Are you mad?"

"Perhaps, but there is method to my madness and necessity is the mother of invention."

Jane stood quite still, then cocked her head to one side. "I heard something."

"It's nothing, pure imagination. You truly are an artist," said the Baron holding tightly to his nerve.

Jane started. "I heard it again, a muffled sound."

"A creaking, groaning sound," said the Baron. "The floor boards settling in for the night, the window frame adjusting, the beating of my feet."

"Your feet?"

"That's where my heart is right now. Will you please get started?" The Baron threw the brocade over himself.

Somehow his fear set Jane's at rest. She glued the fabric around his head, his chest, his arms, his legs, and selected magic markers from the drawers. "I work fastest in my specialty, but you won't look very pretty," she said, as she began to outline his form.

"Good! Let me be all knuckles and elbows for a change," came the somewhat garbled reply.

"And oh," his face popped out from an edge of the brocade, "thanks a lot!"

Jane sketched his features quickly — triangular eyes, a square nose, electric-wave lips, hexagonal ears, and three conical roll-up chins. In his right hand she drew a nightcap with a tassel.

"You're done."

From somewhere came the creak and the groan, from somewhere, but not from the Baron. Jane sucked in her breath. The Baron made neither movement nor sound.

"Baron?" Her voice was unsteady.

Gingerly she extended her fingers to the brocade. The fabric collapsed into itself onto the floor. Frightened, Jane drew back.

"I've killed the Baron," she thought. "Heaven above, I've killed the Baron!"

She had a fleeting thought of draping the brocade over the lampshade and repainting the Baron as he had been. Repainting him from memory. Repainting him with accuracy, with fidelity to what he had been. Could she do it? Her hands shook.

"I've killed the Baron!" She sank onto the sofa.

Jane was aroused from her shock and paralysis by a loud thump. It had come from the wall behind her. She stared briefly at the wall, then got to her feet and headed for the door, resolved to investigate. She paused there to look with sinking heart at what had once been Baron Kisonauf. She picked him up, draping the brocade about her shoulders.

"Together," she whispered, "for better, for worse. Come on!"

The room next door was a bedroom, a powder-puff, lilac and lace bedroom, and in the bed, unceremoniously trussed and gagged, was General Burgoyne.

"IT FIGURES. HE HAD A THUMPING REPUTATION IN BED."

Jane wasn't amused. Where had that thought come from?

★★★★★

Monsieur le Marquis scanned the Court for the third time. He hesitated to ask Madame de Veneer if she had seen Jane. She had a direct line to his mother. He had last seen Jane half an hour earlier, still in the company of Baron Kisonauf. Monsieur le Marquis could not avoid an unflattering judgment on her taste. He felt no sympathy for the Baron, who had failed where he had succeeded. The Baron's behavior had been mere parody of love, lacking in convincing ardor and drained of originality by repetition and rote. The Baron had been and continued to be a fool. It did not occur to the Marquis that to some eyes perhaps he was, too. He sat on a bench to ponder his problem. He had been entrusted with the care of Jane Blaiser, to escort her and exhort her to enjoy this evening, with a view to saving her marriage. How, he did not know. The thought still rankled. Mother had seen fit to inform that wooden-headed feather duster Madame de Veneer, but not her own son. He was fed up with his clothes, fed up with this pose. Lady Hamilton had whet his appetite for different games this night. "Damn! The inconvenience of discipline."

He got up and strode moodily to the hall. Excitement, adventure — would Jane Blaiser lead him to that, or was this humdrum affair penance for his last unsanctioned escapade? His mother simply did not appreciate him, and his father had better things to do, so he said, though what could possibly be better than a lifetime of dalliance and love the Marquis could not imagine. He opened the door and looked out onto the street. He felt a sudden desire to race down it into the heart of the city, wreaking havoc of the most exemplary sort — bringing unknown lovers face to face with the light in each other's eyes, causing paper flowers planted in sidewalk pots to bloom, turning tulips into a blaze of azaleas, scattering crocus petals like confetti down the most unassuming street, and gathering rain in one tremendous watering can and sprinkling water heady with the fragrance of love over the entire unnatural, love-starved, concrete metropolis.

The Marquis sighed. "There's a humanitarian itch behind this cupidity of mine. I wish Mother understood me better."

He looked at the street before him. Across the way a tree sported a thin spread of leaves. He looked up. The only flowers to be seen were on the drapes in a second floor Frick window, faintly illuminated by a yellow street light. The second floor. The Marquis turned away. He walked down the East Vestibule and into the South Hall, stopping before the staircase. He put his hand on the banister and started up the stairs.

★★★★★

Jane struggled with the ropes that bound the General, while he regaled her with a recitation of the events leading up to THE event. Saint Jerome had lured him upstairs with a story about a damsel in distress, had broached the proposition of an exchange of identities, and after being roundly refused, had hit him on the head with a cosmetics case and placed him in his present position.

"I was flattered at the compliment he paid my acting ability, but appalled to think he could imagine that I, that anyone, would care to play a saint."

The General was free now. He rubbed his wrists and ankles. "What a twist, to be rescued by a beautiful lady. Jane Blaiser, resident of the first dimension, I am gratified." He kissed her hand.

"You know me?"

"Only by inquiry. When I see a beautiful lady, I always make an inquiry."

She carefully extracted her hand, which he had appropriated, from his. "Then Saint Jerome is impersonating you downstairs. Are you going to confront him?"

She was maddeningly practical, thought the General. "Saint Jerome has better taste than he has ascribed to me. Two General Burgoynes! What an incredibly delicious world it would be! Only, of course, Saint Jerome would fluff his part."

"THE PLAY'S THE THING, BUT MYSTERY OR MIRACLE, NOT RING-A-DING-DING."

"Did you say something?"

Jane looked decidedly uncomfortable. "Not a thing. Actually, he's carrying it off quite well. No one seems to suspect the truth."

"I can't believe that. They're pretending. They're laughing at him when he turns away. They must be. I'm going to see."

"Like that?"

"Why not? I'll show that bearded dandy up for what he is."

"A STRONG, DARING, DRAMATIC MAN OF THE CLOTH, YOU SOP. OH, FORGIVE ME VENUS, EXCEPT FOR SOP."

The General looked around uncomfortably. "On the other hand, the situation might prove embarrassing — to him that is. I will remain a gentleman, despite a contrary temptation."

"That's generous of you, General."

"Thank you."

"OH, BOSH!"

"I'll need a disguise," he said thoughtfully, pacing the room. He eyed the brocade, and Jane pulled it more tightly around her shoulders.

"There must be something suitable in this closet," she said, walking quickly toward it.

"Female things." The General grimaced, then beamed. "What a lark! Imagine playing up to the old devil. Well, if he's playing me he's no saint!"

Jane shook her head vigorously. "We'll have nothing to do with such a scheme."

"We?"

The door opened.

The General was not pleased. "Was that your cue, Marquis? I've always found timing most important in everything I do."

The Marquis frowned. "You haven't changed a bit, Baron."

"Well, thank you, but — great Venus! You don't think I'm that ninny Baron Kisonauf!!"

"It takes one to know one," said Jane. She turned red. "I'm sorry, did I say that?"

"Yes, and most appropriately so," said the Marquis. "I've missed you."

"Did you? Wasn't Lady Hamilton alluring enough?"

General Burgoyne laughed. "You haven't changed a bit, Amour!"

The Marquis ignored him. "Supper will be served in a quarter of an hour. If we hurry, we can get in a dance or two before the feast begins."

Jane's mouth opened. "If music be the food of love, play on."

The General gushed, "Give me excess of it."

The Marquis put an arm through Jane's. "You, Baron, are a lascivious old coot!"

"Amour! Don't you know me, Amour? The Baron is plying his deceitful trade again, and now on you. It's me, General Burgoyne, truly!"

"As you would say, Baron, never judge a book by its cover."

"Never," Jane struggled to hold back the words, "never judge a book by its cover. Just love it, love it." She exhaled deeply.

The Marquis shook his head. "There must be a full moon. You can't be *this* powerful, Baron. Jane, you're with me for the night. Come."

"I'm glad you remembered. But now it's my turn to forget. I've thrown in my towel with the Baron, the real Baron."

"You can't do this to me! What will Mother say?"

"What everyone says, that love is blind. I'm tired of being told what to do, and what to say. Yes, yes," she said, wringing the neck of the brocade clinging to her shoulders, "what to say, too! I'm me, myself! I'm nobody else! I'm not a prop in a game of charades!"

There was a moment of silence. The General and the Marquis stared dumbly at her. Her anger turned to a scowl, her scowl to a grin, and her grin to uproarious laughter. It gradually subsided, and she shook her head at both of them.

"So," she said, "You think that all the world's a stage and all the men and women merely players, that they have their exits and their entrances?" And leaving the question hanging in the air, she flounced from the room.

"I'M RATHER A MILLSTONE AROUND YOUR NECK AND SHOULDERS. FORGIVE ME."

"Dear Baron, you are forgiven. We'll go down and unwig Madame de Veneer. It's the least I can do for you. It will be a deed of kindness."

The Baron made no response, and Jane half-regretted the remark. She wished she could see his face.

"I'm glad you haven't disappeared completely. What happened?"

"I'M GLAD TOO. I DON'T KNOW, UNLESS VENUS IS ONE STEP AHEAD OF ME. MAYBE I'LL MATERIALIZE YET BEFORE THE NIGHT IS OVER."

"What if you don't? What if the party ends and you're still in this condition? What — what will become of you?"

"I'D RATHER NOT THINK ABOUT THAT JUST NOW. LET'S LIVE IN HOPE, SHALL WE, EVEN IF IT'S ONLY FOR A MATTER OF HOURS. I CAME HERE IN HOPE, AND I FOUND YOU. THERE'S HOPE. IT SPRINGS ETERNAL."

Jane threw him a mournful look.

"AS IT SHOULD!" insisted the Baron. They were in the East Vestibule now. "DO WE FOLLOW OUR PLAN, OR WING IT?"

Jane thought of the diligent artist she had been, of her tutelage under Eric Ludwig, of the gallery she had so painstakingly established, of winning Alan. Plans and schemes. Enough.

"Let's try our wings."

She walked through the mansion with the Baron. It was in the Oval Room that she spotted Madame de Veneer.

"Madame de Veneer, have you seen Baron Kisonauf?"

"No, my dear; why would I want to do that? Have you met Miss Edwards?"

"No. How do you do?"

"Jane is charmingly formal, Mary. So unlike the women of her time. Jane Blaiser is an art person, and very much up on our guests, I'm afraid. She probably knows all about you, so you may speak freely."

"As you know I do. You must be special, Jane, because you are not one of us. What brings you here?"

"It's an honor I don't deserve and don't quite understand. But Madame de Veneer isn't one of you either, though obviously a very special person."

"Very special," said Mary Edwards, looking at the de Veneer headdress. "There's a naked green ostrich running around somewhere."

"Mary, you young reprobate, lucky for you I don't take you seriously."

Mary Edwards laughed. "Now that stunning white brocade shawl of Jane's is unique. Can you compare the craftsmanship of that to your feathers?"

"Stunning, my foot! It looks like a bedspread."

"It is a bedspread," said Jane.

"Oh, yes, I've heard about such things," said Miss Edwards with interest. These days bath towels are used as curtains, tablecloths, even clothes."

"Not clothes, quite yet," said Jane.

"Too bad. I like new things"

"Like men," said Madame de Veneer.

"Always the gracious hostess," said Miss Edwards. "Is your shawl lined, Jane?"

Jane removed it for Miss Edwards' examination.

"Um, lovely." She ran her hand over the material. "But what's this? Did you paint this yourself? Here, Cynthia, look at this." She offered part of the fabric to Madame de Veneer.

"Yes, I painted it myself. It's a man."

"Thanks for telling us." Miss Edwards unfurrowed her brow.

"Any special reason you wanted this particular man on your back?" asked Madame de Veneer.

"I took a liking to him."

"Ah, General," said Madame de Veneer to General Burgoyne who was hovering near, "did you hear that? You've lost your battle for Mademoiselle Blaiser to the Man of Brocade. Will you accept your defeat, General?"

"Never!" thundered the General. "I cannot permit beauty to waste itself on a man of cloth. Naturally, were he a man of *the* cloth, I would defer."

"Well, that would certainly be turning over a new leaf," said Madame de Veneer

"Fig," said Miss Edwards.

"Madame de Veneer, if I may say so," said Jane, "your expressions have begun to parallel those of Baron Kisonauf."

"Oh, that odious man! Perish the thought!"

Mary Edwards was gleeful. "You've gone and done it, Cynthia! 'Perish the thought' indeed!"

"You've both conspired to vex me, but that repugnant creature must be near to have polluted my conversation so."

"I didn't know he had that kind of power," said Miss Edwards.

"He hasn't," she responded with assurance, "not a bit."

"Every dog has his day," Jane said matter-of-factly.

"You!" exclaimed Madame de Veneer.

"The spittin' image."

Miss Edwards laughed. "Don't pull her leg, Jane. Oh my, now I'm doing it!"

Madame de Veneer stared in horror at Mary Edwards. "No, no, don't come near me, either of you!" Her eyes blazed as she backed away from them, turned, and fled.

The brocade, once more in Jane's possession, seemed a burden now, heavy on her back and shoulders. From somewhere within her came the call to follow her hostess. She picked her way among the guests, following the path of the green headdress.

HURRY, HURRY, JANE. ONCE SHE REACHES THE GARDEN IT WILL BE TOO LATE.

She felt the words press her body. Too late, too late. The words carried her forward with all the ardor of blind regret for things done and undone and things yet to be. Madame de Veneer had almost reached the garden doors, and Jane, a dozen steps behind, in desperation and panic loudly called her name.

Madame stumbled on the topmost step. Her head flew back, hurling her headdress behind her. Jane swung the brocade over her head, and in the resulting sling caught the feathered piece. The weight brought her to her knees. Looking up she saw Madame de Veneer shout, fling out her arms, and fall headlong down the stairs. There was no sign of her at the foot of the stairs.

"She's probably rolled under a bush."

Jane jumped back at the sight of the figure at her side.

"Don't be afraid. I'm your doing, you know."

"Baron, Baron!" She hugged the material. "You've come alive, you're all right!"

"I'm better, thank you, Help me look for our hostess."

Madame de Veneer was found in parts: head here; arms here and there; legs yonder and beyonder; torso, moreso.

Jane shuddered.

"It's all right," said the Baron, holding up the torso. It was of smoothly polished wood as was the rest of her. "A puppet, a puppet without strings, like your wireless, you know. Venus is always ahead of the times."

He saw her look of wonder and dismay.

"Oh, don't worry. Unlike Humpty Dumpty, Madame de Veneer can be put together again and will be, the next time Venus needs her."

"I wonder what it was she shouted before she fell?"

"Probably something about her clothes."

"Yes, where have they gone to, I wonder?"

"The same place yours have, I would imagine."

Jane looked down. She was naked.

"I'm sorry you can't wrap yourself in me anymore. I've got to stand as a separate person. But take heart, you look great, and" — his eyes took in the scene indoors — "you've got plenty of company."

It was Garden of Eden night at the Frick.

"Good heavens, we can't go in there!"

"Why not? I will."

"Oh, it's fine for you to talk; you're just a piece of fabric."

"And what a time to be in this state," he sighed. "White, yet! Blander I couldn't look."

"Baron, be a dear. Go inside and find me some fabric to drape around myself."

"I don't think that's the way it's supposed to be. When in the Frick, do as the Frickeans do. Anyway, every piece of cloth has probably been nailed down or turned to stone. Venus doesn't botch a job. I'd be in your condition too, if Venus had conjured up my clothes."

"Then I'm staying out here, forever, if necessary!"

"And you call yourself an artist?"

"But this is not a painting. What will those people think?"

"Oh, they've been stripped of more than their clothes. They've been stripped of all conventional thoughts and actions. You see them now as they really are."

Jane strained at the view inside.

"Come a little closer. That's right. Now wouldn't it amuse you to see what these people are truly like from an objective point of view, since you are here, since dinner is about to be served, and since I'm starved?" He took her arm and led her reluctantly up the stairs and through a pair of double doors.

Jane had no opportunity to be embarrassed. Her gaze immediately fastened on the cherubic face and rounded contours of Bunny. He met her glance with a familiar, approving one of his own. She became aware of a pulling on her arm. The thought vaguely floated to her that a ridiculous appurtenance was attaching itself to her, but she would not look and she would not let go.

Bunny approached her in rotund dignity. He got down on one knee.

"My humble apology for my despicable desertion earlier this evening. If you could find it in your" — he gazed ahead — "in your heart to forgive me, I will satisfy your every wish to the best of my considerable ability." He remained kneeling.

"I think it's perspective rather than humility that keeps you on your knees," rasped the Baron.

Bunny rose. He eyed Baron Kisonauf with distaste. "Pardon me, Your Ghostliness."

The Baron spoke strongly, and several bodies turned to look at him. "I am The Cloth Man. You are the offspring of Love. One never knows how one's offspring will turn out, does one?"

Bunny eyed him maliciously, which look the Baron quite effectively returned.

"The Cloth Man, eh?"

"You think Stuffed Shirt is more like it?"

Bunny grinned.

"I'm good material, elegant, elaborate, tough."

Bunny chuckled and slapped him on the back.

"May we?" they asked in chorus. Each offered Jane an arm.

"Mai oui!" she responded.

Her eyes rose above her fleshly surroundings, but gradually, as the trio made its way through the Hall, she lowered them. The activity was unexpected, and by the time she arrived at the Court, unnerving. It was frenzied, manic, and mainly in the eyes. Hands, as though lethargic, slowly wound their way over hillocks and mountains, through thickets and around wickets, circumnavigating with care each globe.

"It's the thought that counts," said The Cloth Man, bending low in a bow as the Marquis pulled out her chair for Jane.

Lavender birds flew in with the appetizer, glistening salads on gold trays. Some indefinable music wafted through the room like a cool breeze, and everyone beamed at everyone else. Only General Burgoyne looked unhappy. No voices cut into the music, no dinnerware clattered, no menus were cracklingly fingered, no hands were on the table.

A procession of white birds flew in with the fruit soup. Rich, red, ripe strawberries flecked their own snowy sour cream broth. The chill mingled with the steam. There was confusion and resistance. Lady Peel slapped the real General Burgoyne so hard he fell off his chair. Mary Edwards threw her soup at Don Pedro, and Lady Hamilton pummeled his back and pulled his hair as The Polish Rider rode.

Mountains of wine-soaked beef were served on flame-encircled trays by pink birds that flew in and out on silent wings. The heat steamed the air, permeating it with an aromatic fog. And everyone beamed at everyone else. Senseless, thought Jane, as she beamed too.

Dessert appeared from nowhere, as dessert so often does. Rainbow slices of cake with surprises inside: orange pistachios coated with ice cream, blue banana tidbits whirled in a whipped cream mix, apple shavings encircling walnut purée, and beside each dish a carafe of red wine. There was friendly consultation and a sampling of dishes, with nods, smiles and satisfied murmurs for the laden plates, the hot, spicy wine, the mortal morsels. The diners gorged themselves in floating on its Venusian tide. Jane's eyes had widened briefly at the start, but lust was not an unfamiliar sight. It made a kind of senseless sense, and she watched, more in awe than surprise, as Bunny and the Baron fended off the follow-ups to the leers and lascivious looks to which she was subjected. Her guardians were on their guard, the officially appointed and the self-appointed. She smiled at the creaseless fabric that was the Baron, at the wall of brocade, and ran her hand affectionately down his arm.

Jane viewed the proceedings with objective abandon. Most of the guests had opted for a piece of flesh — an arm, a buttock, a nipple, a thigh — many for two and some for an octopi-like assortment utilizing all the feelers at their disposal. The women vied, unabashedly and successfully, with the men. All was thrashing arms and legs, like turbulence at sea during a storm.

"When will this damned orgy end?" muttered the Marquis.

"Then you don't like it?" asked Jane in surprise.

He shrugged. "It's all right."

"Too many cooks spoil the broth," volunteered the Baron. "A finger in every pie at once is not to my taste either."

"Since when?" asked the Marquis de L'Amour.

The Baron was silent.

Above the heavy breathing and muted shrieks sounded a siren, a piercing soprano. It grew in strength and intensity until it alone was audible. The Marquis held his naked sides and laughed.

"It's wonderful, wonderful! Leave it to Mother!"

Naked people scattered throughout the ground floor of the mansion. Then, as the front door burst open, the naked horde, parts flopping, poured into the street, mowing down the raiding party.

"Wonderful, wonderful!" Bunny clapped his hands and jumped like a jack rabbit. "I can see tomorrow's headlines: ORGY AT FRICK, HUNDREDS ARRESTED, PAINTINGS STOLEN."

He made a dash for the library, pulling Jane who pulled the Baron. "There's a foolproof place to hide," he blurted gleefully. "Isn't Mother wonderful?"

A woman rose from behind the library desk. "And this is the way you repay her," stated Sergeant Weller flatly.

The Marquis de L'Amour stared at the woman before him. "Mother is a sh–thead!" he said.

Chapter Seven

ALAN BLAISER SAT FACING HIS wife. He said nothing, but looked at her expectantly. She sat with her hands in her lap, where she had placed them after wrenching them free from Alan's and putting him in his place, a distance away from her.

"I did nothing wrong, and I won't be treated as if I did, especially by my husband. I shouldn't require a lawyer, and I definitely don't require to be picked up by a lady cop with whom you seem to be on friendly terms."

"We are not friendly and you haven't seen her walking around naked."

"Have you?"

"You know I haven't, so don't change the subject. You must have an explanation for last night."

"I know nothing of the sort," Jane said stubbornly, ignoring the second half of his statement.

"Jane, I love you. I want to know why you were at the Frick after closing hours and in *that* condition."

She said nothing.

Alan heaved a deep sigh. "Here comes Gilbey. Confidences between a lawyer and his client and all that … At least talk to *him*. I just want — " He struggled and gave up. "Jack Gilbey, my wife Jane. I'll be in the kitchen, if you need me."

"Mrs. Blaiser, finally, the real Jane Blaiser, I'm here to help you."

Jane laughed a mocking laugh, and through Gilbey's mind there flashed the vision of Adele Munson and her threat to do likewise. He certainly deserved better than that, he felt.

"My dear, the law does not take what occurred last night lightly. Surely you don't want to spend time in some horrid old jail cell and part with some of your merited earnings as penalty for something quite harmless and innocent. And your reputation! You are a business woman. Can you afford a scandal?"

Jane nodded. "You're very persuasive, Mr. Gilbey. Divorce law is your specialty, isn't it?"

"Yes it is," he said humbly.

"Out in California, aren't you?"

"Yes."

"Flew in on business, didn't you? Impending divorce? Secret meetings? Spouse in the dark? Correct?"

"Then Alan's told you about it, that rascal. I'm surprised. Well, I guess you two don't have secrets from each other. That's a wonderful way to proceed."

Jane's throat contracted. She waited for the feeling to pass. Gilbey was speaking; she did not know of what. She fought to open her throat and to keep the tears from rolling down her cheeks. She turned her face away from him.

"Ah, I see," he said softly. "Giving him back some of his own. Well, perhaps it's for the best. Adultery is a great equalizer."

She turned on him in fury. "Get out of here! Get out! I want Bunny!" She stormed up and down the room, and when she stopped Gilbey was gone. "Gilbey!" she whispered. "Alan said the Munsons — yes, it was the Munsons — had stolen his precious Gilbey, his precious replacement for Byron. Liar! Liar!" She sank down on the sofa as she heard Alan confronting the attorney. "What's the use," she thought, "it's all over."

Alan burst into the room "What did that idiot Gilbey tell you?"

"Plenty. What you should have told me to my face. It's Sergeant Weller, isn't it?"

"Sergeant Weller? What are you talking about?"

"Gilbey told me all about it, so you can at least be honest with me now. How long have you been seeing her? How did you meet her, anyway? Why would you want someone like that? What makes her so special?"

"If Gilbey told you I've been seeing Ann Weller, he's a damned liar!"

"Ann. It's a pretty name."

"I don't believe this. Why am I arguing about nonsense with you. You were caught without your clothes on at the Frick. That was a real, an indisputable fact. If you won't talk to this lawyer I'll get you another."

"I'd rather you got me Bunny."

"Your Bunny is still in jail."

"You said you'd get him out on bail."

"I forgot."

"Do it now, will you? I've got a cruel headache. I'm going to take a nap. Wake me when he comes."

"But you haven't had a bite to eat. I'll make you some tea, some toast. You must get something in your stomach."

Jane smiled wanly. "The patient had a little something at the Frick. You *will* wake me when Bunny gets here, won't you?"

Jane touched her head to the pillow in relief, although the throbbing in her head continued. It was all so far away now, so unreal — the Baron, the General, Madame de Veneer, the Frick — but she hadn't dreamed it, no. She knew that. Yet it was all so ridiculous, too ridiculous to be real. The elaborate party with the layered look: layers of mask, layers of flesh, layers of silence, and layers of speech. The puppet-run social milieu, the cream of society from off the walls, the Christian and the pagan camps fighting over a woman lost to both. Ridiculous! The mindful and the mindless merging on common ground. Stupid, crazy, unreal. Except for the Baron, the dear, determined Baron. Cloth and all, storybook eyes and all, he had been real. In a short while he would not be coming to her. Coming instead would be Bunny of the adorable body, the Marquis de L'Amour. She could go to the Frick, if they ever let her in again, and look in vain for the Baron's image on the walls. He had crumpled to the floor in a heap when she and Bunny had been led from the Frick. Perhaps he had been thrown into a rag pile, or been used to dust the furniture, or been thrown away. She didn't know. All she knew with the certainty of intuition was that he was gone from her life. Baron Kisonauf was gone, his search a failure, his mission incomplete.

"You see, Baron," she said softly, "there was no hope." She closed her eyes.

★★★★★

"Your husband's a brick. Are you all right?"

Jane raised herself on one elbow and nodded her all-rightness. "What happened to the Baron?"

"Never mind the Baron. The humiliation, the degradation — being carted away like a common criminal, belong photographed like a freak — and it's all Mother's fault! To do such a thing to her son, her *only* son! Don't only children get privileged treatment anymore? What are parents coming to these days? And what did I do. Tell me that. Have you seen the morning papers?" He tossed them on the bed.

The photographer had caught Jane's baffled stare as she was led, wrapped in an oversized coat, to the police van, followed by the blanket-headed Bunny.

"Well, I've got more to lose than you," Bunny said self-righteously. "My reputation could be shattered, if this news reaches my peers. I'd be the laughing stock of mythology. You'll gain plenty. Art lovers will descend like an avalanche on your gallery. Tradition meets modern art. Gallery owner and her strange, surreal cloth escort invade the Frick!"

Jane looked at the front-page story:

"A river of nudity flowed from the Frick and then dried up. When police invaded the mansion, they and witnesses state, the nude figures, reportedly engaging in an orgy at the Frick, left the premises in a rush and were promptly swallowed up by the air. This was amended to 'and vanished as they ran down the street,' which was further amended to 'and ran down the street and disappeared as they rounded the corner.' No paintings from the Collection have been removed or damaged. The only signs of any untoward activity in the mansion were the presence of the nude man and woman apprehended and the otherwise unverified report of goings on by a young woman in a blue satin dress whom the police decline to identify. The woman has disappeared as well. Jane Blaiser, prominent gallery owner —"

"I can't bear to read anymore!"

"'Decline to identify'" repeated Bunny mockingly. They couldn't pronounce her name even if they knew it."

"The Comtesse d'Haussonville!"

"The Comtesse, all right. She must have thought she was writing one of her books! I'm disappointed in her. When I heard her sweet voice last night —"

"Yes, that's the way I imagined it would be, but it was very hoarse when the Baron and I spoke to her."

"Well, really! So that's why Saint Francis sounded like a songbird. I thought he'd been drinking! Well, he and the Comtesse have had their fun. One up for God."

"Can't you just disappear? You don't have to go through all this earthly nonsense, do you?"

"Run out on Mother? Not a chance. The last time I did that she ruined every fun project I arranged for a year. Not that Mother carries a grudge, just a nudge. It's enough."

"And all for love. But there's no rushing love, is there. It takes a long time to grow and a long time to go."

"Outside of a few freaks like Romeo and Juliet, I agree, but we eternal children are willing to settle for that traumatic substitute while waiting for the real thing. Passion's no mere fashion, and as the ad says, 'Getting there is half the fun.' Maybe more."

Jane smiled faintly. "That's what the Baron would have said — once."

"The Baron, the Baron! What's the matter with me?"

"I don't know. I guess it's just that — you don't need me."

"At this moment, I sure as Jove need somebody!"

"Maybe so, but not me."

"Well, *you need me;* Mother has decreed so. I am the means to your happy ending, so have a little more respect for your romantic tool."

Jane smiled again "I hope you won't be disappointed."

"How about a little jealousy. That should make your husband rush panting to your side."

Jane shook her head. "No good. I've no time for heavy breathing in my ears; I've got a business to run. Anyway, he's already tried the jealousy routine on me."

"Did it work?"

"Yes, but the wrong way. I've still got work to do. He's only made me angry."

Bunny was silent. He stood, his hands behind his back, looking out the window at a man on a park bench. He wheeled around. "You're not my type at all." He walked up and down the room. "Who's the competition?"

"Sergeant Weller. I — I don't know how far it's gone. She — she was at his office the other day looking quite — attractive. Something about a raid of personnel."

"Well, we'd better get the facts first before we act. Stay here and rest. I'll do a little personal investigating. Lovely word 'personal.' Why don't you work up some synonyms for it while I'm gone?"

"Alan will have you followed, if he sees you leave."

"Surely you don't expect me to leave the ordinary way. Relax. Think 'personal.' " He patted her on the arm and was gone.

Jane sighed. "Personal: personal, singular; exclusive, esoteric, private, intimate, erotic — Honestly, that Bunny must be the world's greatest busybody. 'Personal' indeed!"

★★★★★

The ringing of his telephone, the light on his intercom, and the knocking on his door made no impression on Don Byron, who sat behind his huge mahogany desk and looked into space. It had been cruel of Alan and obscene of Ann. He had judged poorly. Yet, it hadn't been her fault, really. She hadn't led him on. He had done that quite nicely himself, romantic fool that he was. But to break with him this way, so ostentatiously, so cruelly, this was unbearable, unbelievable. This was not Ann. Yet there they were — her clothes, the clothes that belonged to the body he loved, there they were in Alan's closet, the case he had seen delivered to his boss's office tucked neatly under the dress suit Alan kept there for emergencies. Still, he had thought him more a gentleman. He had not expected this from either of them. Ann couldn't wait; she had to give Alan Blaiser the ammunition for revenge. "The End" — without justice, without poetry. He thought fleetingly of Mrs. Blaiser. With Alan it had always been Jane this and Jane that. What a cover! He wondered if she knew. Jane Blaiser, now what did she look like? Had he seen her once? He couldn't remember. She had never attended business parties, not that he could recall. Had Alan been hiding her as he had tried to hide Ann? Was she as impossibly precious and beautiful to Alan as Ann was to him? Or did his business simply bore her; was she too busy with her own to bother about his? Yes, Alan had once said as much, hadn't he? Ann —his mind was full of Ann. Who else, what else mattered? The telephone no longer rang, and whoever had been knocking at his door had stopped, but the light on his intercom was still lit. Reluctantly, he responded.

"Yes? Jane who? She what? No, I can't. Make that a great big definite no."

Don Byron leaned back in his chair, "Mind your own business, Byron," he told himself. He lurched forward. "But damn it," he thought, "this is my business. I should have said yes. Arrangements could have been made. In a fit of jealousy Alan would drop Ann and rush to reclaim his Jane, leaving Donald Kendrick Byron in full possession of Ann Weller. If she chose to come back. If he chose to take her back." He creased his brows. "A happy ending." He got out of his chair and paced the floor. "Perhaps it would be more appropriate to suffer."

★★★★★

The Marquis de L'Amour perched on a window sill of the building across the street. He saw Don Byron pacing and Alan Blaiser making like an executive at his office desk.

"Just like children," he murmured. "Let's play president, let's play poet. I prefer post office and house myself." He shivered slightly. "Mother could have picked June." Goose pimples rose on his smooth, naked chest. The quiver of arrows hung lightly over one shoulder, the bow resting in his lap. "A waste of good arrows. A waste of my time." He recalled that he had promised Jane an investigation and that he had promised his mother blind devotion to a happy resolution of this — this — well, whatever you called it. An imposition on his happiness, that's what it was, and it was so unnecessary; the entire complicated, convoluted nonsense could be dispensed with and a sensible solution imposed.

"A happy ending is desired; a happy ending is on the way, not quite as Mother wished, but happiness is happiness, and Jane Blaiser will be happy. Don, Alan, it's time to find yourselves women who appreciate you." The Marquis de L'Amour stretched his pudgy body tall and poised on the window ledge high above the city below. "It's for your own good, too," he addressed the sky grandly, as he set arrow to bow and shot and shot again.

★★★★★

Jane Blaiser stormed away from the window. This couldn't go on; it had to stop. She fingered the intercom.

"Angie, call the police. I want the entrance to this building cleared."

"Mrs. Blaiser, those people are not blocking the entrance and they're not bothering anybody."

"They're bothering me."

"Don't look out the window. Do your work."

Jane nodded. "Thank you, Angie. Forget the police."

Her gallery was filled these days at all hours. That was good. The curious gathered outside at the hour she presumably went out for lunch. She rarely went out for lunch. That was good, too.

Was she getting notoriety or popularity? It didn't matter. "Do your work. Angie is right."

She would work until three and make it an early day. Since the shameful adventure of last week she had had to force herself to grind through the gallery day. What had been love had become duty. Disbelief at what had happened mingled with distaste at her involvement and an almost palpable fear of impending doom in her relations with Alan. Not that she had noticed a change in him. That was what was frightening. He seemed to be the same Alan. And yet there was Ann Weller, and there was her world turned upside down. In time the worry would pass, and the fear would resolve itself into certainty of some sort. She had only to wait for that, to go through an agonizing wait for that. She hoped it would not be long. Meanwhile she had to close her mind to it or she would go mad. She was glad that Vanessa had, as she put it, "imposed" upon her time with a request for help, grateful she could busy herself with someone else's problems instead of her own. That ridiculous-looking Vanessa. Well, she wouldn't look ridiculous after their shopping spree today. She'd wow every man in sight. Keeping them would be another matter.

"You're on your own there," Jane thought, and felt the cruelty of what she was about to begin.

★★★★★

"These things happen," said Byron to Alan, "and with a marquis by the name of Bunny. Of course, of course. They happen all the time, mismatches, like Ann and me. Well, what can you do? If they happen, they happen. You don't dry up and die. You look around. It may be the best thing that could have happened to both of you, to both of us. When I thought you and Ann had something going, it set me thinking. I don't mean to brag, but I'm worth appreciating, and if double flips and back somersaults for a woman don't get appreciation, well, why do them for her? Why not save them for someone who recognizes their value? We've got to find ourselves women who deserve us."

Alan straightened perceptibly. "How do we begin?"

"The elegant way, the gentlemanly way, the right way — by introduction, of course. That was how I met Ann. We were introduced by the arresting officer. Dreadful mistake. My arrest, I mean. And on reflection, maybe the introduction, too. Still, it's the best way to begin. It certainly beats bars and pickups."

"Whom shall we ask?"

"That depends on the kind of woman you're looking for."

"Homebody, clinging vine type."

"Say, I hope we're not going to have a conflict of interest on this."

"I'm sure there is more than one vine in this city. Anyway, I like honeysuckle."

"And I like wisteria, so that's settled. But I threw away my little black book a week after I met Ann."

"Mine is long gone, too."

"Then let's ask them. They ought to know all sorts of women."

"Who?"

"Your spouse and my once-intended."

"That could be dangerous."

"Could be and could be not. After all, our gals have lost interest in us. Granted, that doesn't mean they'll be willing to distribute us generously among their more suitable acquaintances, but what can we lose by asking?"

They turned the corner.

"There's Jane now, but she's with someone."

"Shall we trail them?" Byron asked conspiratorially. "Yes, let's," he answered himself quickly. "We're starting an adventure, friend. Let's start it in style."

At Saks Fifth Avenue Jane's companion shed her bulky coat and acquired a long, crocheted vest, at Lord & Taylor she exchanged a gray suit for a flowered dress pinched at the waist, after Elizabeth Arden her long straight hair waved layer by layer in the light breeze, and at B. Altman her walking shoes changed to peek-a-boo leather atop wood stacks.

"Vanessa!" exclaimed Alan, as he approached the duo. "You look so — so — different!" He beamed.

"Thank you, or rather, thank your wife She thinks men will notice me this way."

"Apparently you've been noticed already," said Jane with a shade of annoyance.

Vanessa laughed. "We met in your gallery. He was waiting for you."

Don Byron cleared his throat.

"Don, this is Vanessa, and this is my wife. Jane, we wanted to ask you —"

"__ if you and your friend would join us for dinner," interjected Don Byron.

"You two seem to have made up your differences," Jane said suspiciously.

"Well, we found our differences were similarities."

"I'm not in a hearty-ho mood. There's too much work to finish at the gallery. I won't have time for any but a paper bag dinner."

"Perhaps a picnic on your desk top?" Byron suggested tentatively. Jane looked aghast.

"That was a joke," explained Byron, drawing himself up to his full six feet.

Vanessa touched Jane's hand and drew back, casting quick glances upward and around her.

The shock faded from Jane's face. "I think I can manage an hour, but I must go back to the office first."

Byron took out two business cards, scribbled something on each, and handed them to the two ladies. "The Magic Pan at six?"

"All right. Vanessa?"

"If you wish."

Byron inclined his head in a simulated bow, Alan waved goodbye, and the two men strode off.

Thick clouds now billowed across the sky and across the sun, casting the street into a garishly lit darkness.

"So you meet Vanessa at The Magic Pan and I meet Jane at The Magic Pan."

"Okay," said Alan absentmindedly. "Look, we'd better hail a taxi or we'll be drenched."

"You've surely been in the rain before," said Byron dryly.

Alan bit his lower lip. "I just don't like this …. There's something, something unnatural …."

"That's because you see it that way. For instance, Jane. I see Jane as more dependent than you do. And that face, that figure! You haven't understood her, but you've had your chance. Vanessa is a very pretty little thing. Good luck."

Alan smiled. "You like challenges, don't you."

"Sometimes. When they're right for me. Jane is right for me."

"And Ann Weller?"

"A happening, just a happening, like this weather."

A stereo crack of thunder shook the ground, throwing Alan off balance.

"You'd better take a taxi back to the office, Alan, or you won't make it. And from only one glass of sherry!" His clicking disapproval was swallowed up by thunder. "Taxi! Taxi!"

Surely only lip reading and hand waving had arrested the attention of the taxi driver, who abruptly halted his vehicle at the side of the two men. The clouds had parted, forming the circumference of a huge hole in the sky, a gigantic black hole from which suddenly gushed forth a hydrant of water over the heads of every scurrying figure in sight, over — as Alan mused before Byron shoved him into the taxi — over the entire world. Byron, his hair now wet-plaster bright, waved gaily as the taxi prepared for takeoff.

"He's celebrating," explained Alan unnecessarily "New lady friend."

The driver grunted. "Could've split the fare."

The taxi lurched into action, but not for long.

"Can't see a damn thing!" yelled the driver, as he swerved to avoid a pedestrian. "Read the street signs for me, will ya buddy? It's all I can do to see what's movin' on the street."

Alan did. For better vision and balance his hands were on the back of the driver's seat. "Don't you think you should slow down a little?"

"You crazy? I wanna get the hell off the street soon as I can." He flicked on his off-duty sign. The car slowed.

"Thanks!" Alan was about to lean back gratefully.

"Oh, for Chrissakes," moaned the cabbie. "Look!"

Alan followed his gaze out the side window and to the road. Through the gush of rain he could see that the water was over the wheels.

"Engine's out. Hell! Why didn't you walk with your friend?"

The rain, which had been straight, now began to blow. The cabbie rolled up most of his window, turned off the engine and took out a cigarette.

"You can't just sit here," protested Alan.

"I sure can, but don't let me stop you from leavin'. That'll be $2.50."

"But we can get rammed sitting here like this!"

The driver turned to look at him quizzically. Any car can ram me in this flood, I say more power to it. This baby's still got a $30,000 mortgage on her, so I'm not abandoning ship."

"Have you got a radio relay or short wave?"

"What if I do? Want me to hail some boob and his car for company?"

Alan glared.

A few minutes and a radioed message later the cabbie leaned back in his seat. Apparently the whole city was inundated. Alan hoped Jane and Vanessa were safe inside somewhere. He wrinkled his brow. The swirling rain made it hard to see anything but the huge, blurred bulk of the buildings on either side. Alan closed his eyes. When he opened them the slashing rain had become a familiar downpour. The water reached to just below the windows. It was now clear that on the street before them and behind them lay a line of traffic. There was no horn beeping, but a lot of head-leaning out of car windows, apartment and office windows and, now that they could be heard, shouts. They were many and inconsequential, centering around the incredibility of the situation and the possibilities of rescue. When the water reached above the car windows, the shouts would decrease.

Alan counted out $2.50 "I should be able to swim to the office. I suggest you swim over to one of these buildings and keep your eye on the cab from someone's window."

"$2.50 and advice. A tip to be treasured."

Alan emptied his pockets of all change. "I can't swim with this anyway. It's impossible for you to stay here; you'll drown with your cab."

The cabbie waved his arms helplessly at the rain "Impossible? So is this!"

Alan secured his wallet and credit cards to the top of his head with his tie knotted under his chin.

The cabbie turned around. "Cute."

"Give me a shove, will you?" Alan had rolled down the window to the water line and, having discarded his jacket, was attempting to squeeze himself through the opening. The cabbie pushed.

Alan swam to the corner and looked around. There was static traffic as far as the eye could see. Store signs and debris floated down the street, interfering with the progress of several other determined-looking swimmers. Faces peered down from every window and rooftop.

"Look out!" Alan's shout aroused attention, but no compliance, as is usual with vague, undirected, imperious commands. A flower pot made a ten stone splash into the Madison Avenue river. When the shower of water had settled, it was obvious that three people had been affected by the fall. Alan swam vigorously toward them. One was bobbing up and down, gasping for breath, another was draped face down over a floating store sign, and a third had disappeared from sight. Alan grabbed the bobber by an arm and in two strokes had him over the floating sign. Then he dove. Seconds later he came up sputtering, holding by the armpits a raven-haired girl with finely chiseled features and a very pale face. The water was now above the tops of the neighboring doorways. There were now three on the raft. The two draped figures lifted their heads to survey the newcomer.

"Are you guys all right?" asked Alan.

"Yes," coughed one. "Fine, fine," wheezed the other.

"Good! Think you can swim alongside this sign and hold it steady?"

They nodded and were in the water again. Alan stretched the woman out on the sign. In a flowing, foamy green and white fabric, flowing somewhat still despite its sopping condition, the lady lay expectant, a sleeping-beauty look upon her face. Mermaids flashed through Alan's mind. Her breathing was shallow. He lifted both her arms straight up in the air. Now, how did it go? He gave up on CPR and pressed his mouth to hers. Business was business.

"Is everybody all right?" came a shout from ten stories up.

"No, get a doctor," one of the signbearers shouted back.

"What?"

"Get a doctor!" his partner shouted. His repetition of the request, made with some exuberance, caused him to allow the craft to tip to one side. The beautiful lady opened her eyes and clasped Alan about the neck as the two of them rolled off into the brown water.

"You need a doctor?" came the shout from above.

"No, no, please," the lady whispered to Alan in a thick Italian accent. They were both clutching the sign now.

"Are you sure? It really would be better —"

"No, no doctor," she insisted, "not here." Bewildered, she looked around at the debris in the water and the spot that held a car that had not yet sunk.

"Yes, of course. Very sensible. Dry land first. Can you swim along with me?"

"Yes." She smiled wanly.

An onslaught of goose pimples attacked Alan. He cupped a hand to his mouth. "It's all right," he shouted to the woman above. "No doctor! She's all right!"

"Did my flower pot crack?"

Alan ignored the question and looked at the young woman. "Follow me Miss, ah —"

"Gina."

"Gina, what's the matter. Can I help you?"

"Yes, you can take me with you. You are an American, yes? Take me home with you. I will be good, I will do what you say."

Alan nearly slid off the sign "What are you talking about? I can't, my wife—"

"You have a wife? But that is no matter to me. I will be your servant for seven years, as it says in the Bible. Then you can let me go. I did not want to live, but you saved my life, It was a sign. Help me, please!"

"Come with me," Alan said softly, "you *do* need a doctor."

"No, no doctor, no!" she screamed, and she turned and swam uptown.

"Wait, Gina wait!" Alan took off after her. He thought of mermaids again, not for face or form, but for aquatic style and skill. Gina submerged and surfaced with speed and grace. "Will you wait!"

"Hey, mister!" Blonde pigtails framed the face at a second floor window. "My bottle of insulin fell out the window. Would you dive for it, please? The bottle's still sealed, so it will be okay."

Alan scanned her face. "So young," he thought. He dove. At the bottom was a mess of dirt and slime and a bottle. He surfaced with it and shook the water from his eyes. The bottle was not insulin.

"That's it. Throw it up, will you?"

"But it's not —"

"Throw it up, anyway. How's your pitching arm?"

He gazed with disapproval at the girl above. Not more than fifteen, he guessed. Alan made a dramatic windup and threw. He heard a clatter of glass and a shriek. An old lady with a shock of blue hair shook her fists and screamed incomprehensively at him, while next to her the girl in pigtails waved.

Alan swam on. Apart from three or four people who said "hi," as they swam past and several who sat glumly, Thinkeresque atop their cars, the streets were empty, observed from on high by those who were dry, still dry. Alan looked up into the rain. Would it never end? At the corner he wiped his face with one hand and came away with some wet paper stuck to it, bits of driver's license and credit cards. He untied the documents on his head and put them inside his shirt. This way, he reasoned, he would at least have the pieces to past together. Gina was gone. He was a fool to allow himself to be sidetracked from his pursuit of her by a silly young girl playing games. Might as well swim back to the office. He did so carefully, diving periodically to detect hidden obstacles ahead — automobiles, upended bicycles — and gingerly picking his way around cans, plastic bottles, and the like bobbing on the surface. He leaned against a lamppost to rest and examined his watch. Next block, ad turf.

"What the —"

Ten o'clock, he read. The church bells chimed four times. Darkness rolled across the sky.

"Except for those waterways outside your front doors, it's sunny and mild, folks, perfect spring weather," blared a radio.

The street light glared into action. Alan shook, shook uncontrollably. He threw his arms around the lamppost, waiting for the tremors to subside.

"Inhale that water-scented air, folks, from your terrace, window sill, or fire escape, but you're urged to stay indoors until the cleanup operation begins, after the sewers have done what they can."

Alan's tremors increased.

"Meanwhile, enjoy the view."

Alan looked down. There was a whirlpool at his feet! He clung tightly to the lamppost. This was insane! He opened his mouth to call out. A huge wave of water set him choking, took his breath away, set his ears ringing. The lamppost was slipping away.

"No! One more block, just —"

"Enjoy, folks, enjoy. Things like this don't happen every day. Temperature: 69, Humidity: 54, Winds: Southwest at one mile per hour, Waters off Sandy Hook: calm. The time is 4:05."

Chapter Eight

To Alan the world was water, blue-black under a faintly lit sky. Water from one horizon to the other and silence, except for the beat of waves against his body. He fought to move, the water brackish in his mouth, but for each stroke forward he was beaten back two. A jumble of thoughts flashed through his mind as he struggled ahead. Then he gave in, let the water toss him where it would, recognized its power, and bent to its will. He did not know how long it had been so before he felt a change. He was no longer tossed, he was cradled, and lying on his back looking at the unchanged sky he wondered if this was the time for him to make a move. He did not decide immediately; his timing had been wrong too often in the past. From the corner of his eye he saw the low profile of buildings nestled in the water. He turned on his stomach and gasped, then swam strongly ahead. The silhouettes rising now on either side left no doubt. He was entering Venice, city of dreams. Avoiding areas directly illumined by the lampposts that rimmed the water's edge, he passed between docked tugboats. Venice! He must be mad! Strollers cast long shadows that almost touched him as he swam uncertainly in the darkness, less unsure of the water at his back than of the movement before him. There was a chorus of girlish laughter punctuated by loud male voices. A soft flow of sound passed quite near him, a paunchy couple nodding, murmuring, and nodding again. Their shadows passed. In the distance music faintly flowered the air. A light breeze blew from the sea. Alan shivered. He was conscious of the wallet pressing against his chest. In the morning it would get him into a sweater and get a big breakfast into him. He was ravenously hungry. Meanwhile … meanwhile what was there to do? He cast appraising eyes at the tugboat nearest him. He couldn't answer questions and he had no passport, or had that miraculously appeared from out of nowhere too? He removed the wallet from his shirt, then replaced it without examining its contents. It was better to wait until tomorrow, until it was dry and he was dry, and the light and his mind were clear and sharp. He eyed the tugboat a while longer, before he heaved himself over the side and onto the deck. It was dark and quiet. He made a brief tour, but found no one. In the pilothouse he found a blanket. He stripped, hung his clothes over the captain's chair, wrapped himself in the blanket, and lay on the floor out of view of the window. The floor was hard and the blanket itched. A hammock would be paradise, he thought. For at least the hundredth time he murmured "Venice!" as the water lapping against the boat lulled him to sleep.

★★★★★

There was a creaking sound in the cabin. Alan moved on the floor. The sound was repeated. Alan sat up and wiped the sleep from his eyes. An old man sat facing him, an unlit pipe in his hands.

"Trouble, alwaysa trouble. You too?"

"I was swimming and I got lost, so —"

"Dadsa ride, dadsa ride. What else? Herea de clothes. You go."

"Yeah, you bet. Thanks." He reached for his wallet.

"Is alla dere. Whad I need trouble from you? Godda trouble my own." He ran his hands through his gray, tousled hair. "Plendy trouble my own, believe me. No can talk," he said reluctantly. "Makea fass; buddin de shird oudside. Mario in a bada mood. Isa cool oud. You take Mario's jacked."

"Yeah, you bet. Thanks, again."

The old man's face cracked into a smile. "Boy! My Englisha bedder dan yours! Yeah, you bet!" He chuckled and opened the door. The morning light was crisp and clear.

"I'm starved. Any safe place to eat nearby?"

"Depens. Who you run away from?"

"I mean is the food safe to eat?"

"I eadda the food alla my life. Sixty-one years. Nodding bedda. You sixty-one? Bud you wanna the bes you ead Luigi's. Nex to de flower stan run by de red lady. Maybe 200 meeders dis way." They crossed the deck, the old man nodding greetings to the workmen boarding the boat.

"You mean red as in sunburn," Alan verified slowly.

This seemed to tickle the old man, whose shoulders heaved as he indulged in silent laughter. "Red as in hair," he responded just as slowly. "Trip to America every year for red hair. Imported, high class, real red." His shoulders heaved again. "Bud gooda business for Luigi. You tell him I send you. He giva you de bes."

Some distance from the boat a muscular man with jet black hair and a plaid shirt rolled up to his armpits waved to the old man, standing now with Alan on the gangplank.

The old man's face darkened. "You scram, scram!"

"Thanks again." Alan sprang down the plank.

The old man watched as Alan passed the muscular man, as they looked at each other. "Safa to ead! Hmph! Americans!" He allowed himself a chuckle, then a sigh of resignation "Alwaysa de trouble, dese young ones." He lit his pipe.

Alan stopped in front of Luigi's. The red lady drew his attention much as would a colorful, ebullient circus performer. She was a tall, buxom woman of about fifty, her hair piled in a high cone. Her peasant clothes were unusual, a disco array of colors that seemed to leap at the viewer every which way with each movement she made, and she was in constant motion, dancing around her flower cart, petting and cooing at her bouquets, seeming almost a part of them and they of her as they swayed and jumped about to her melodic, deep, throaty talk. A small group of chatting people, wallets drawn, surrounded her. She bade a final farewell to a cornucopia of gardenias. Something jogged in Alan's memory for a moment, but it passed.

He surveyed Luigi's. It was a jerry-built looking place, with tumbled-down old world charm on the outside and, he discovered upon entering, sturdy construction and clean tablecloths on the inside. Faded paintings of Rome were neatly squared away from each other on facing, starkly white walls. The paintings mitigated the medicinal look. Alan did not have to sniff; the aromas hitting his nostrils were in no way medicinal.

"Buon Giorno!" A stout man, all smiles, clasped Alan's hands in his. "You sita here" He pulled out a chair at a tiny table facing the antics of the red lady.

"It doesn't matter where I sit. Mario said your food is the best."

"Atsa fo sure, but I'ma surprise to hear him saya so. You knowa him good?"

"Well, no, you see I just got in from New York —"

"Jumpin pasta! You're the cousin from New York!"

Alan dropped the menu. "What happened to your accent?"

His host looked around. The two other patrons, busy with coffee and newspapers, had apparently taken no notice.

"It's strictly for the foreign trade. But that Mario! He still considers us green horns, me and Rita." He pointed to the red lady. "Four years back and we're still not acceptable to Mr. Macho himself, the pure unadulterated Italian. But I run this place as good as Papa did. He'd be proud of what I've done with it. That Mario's a prejudiced pig, but he's right about my food. The best in Venice."

Alan sniffed. "Smells wonderful. What is it?"

"Specialty of the house. You come for lunch; you won't regret it."

"I'm starved. Can I have some now?"

"Are you kidding? It won't be ready 'til noon. Takes four hours to prepare. It's an old family recipe. None of that fast food stuff here. We're not back in the States, you know."

"Why did you come back to Venice?"

"Well, I kinda got fed up. You know, small fish in a big pond getting nowhere, that sort of thing. And Pop had the business and I had two husky boys who like to eat, so ... We get back to New York every year, so we have the best of both worlds. Mario says if you've got two homes you've got none. Narrow-minded as hell, but I like the old man."

"He seems like a nice guy."

"He is, helluva nice guy. But this must be pretty embarrassing for you. I mean, you come to see Gina and you're stuck with Mario."

"Yeah." Alan studied the menu. "Mushroom omelette and potatoes."

"You've got it."

Alan smiled. "The wife doesn't do breakfast?"

"You kidding? My boys wouldn't let her in the kitchen. Not that she'd ever want to go there. She's a modern woman, even in the Old World! Still, Gina wouldn't have run off if she'd known a relative from the States was coming to visit. Better get you your breakfast."

Alan stared after him, then reached into his pocket for his wallet and thumbed through the contents. No passport, of course. He hadn't really expected to find one. It was nice to know there was something one could be sure of. Luigi returned with breakfast.

"I'm worried about Gina," Alan said.

Luigi sat down.

Alan started on the omelette. "She wants me to take her back with me. I want to know why."

"Then you've seen her?" Luigi was excited.

"Well, actually, her letters ..." He trailed off. He was such a bad liar.

Luigi sighed. "Such a beautiful woman, with such long, soft, black hair...."

Alan smiled agreement. "Very beautiful."

Luigi slapped the table. "Aha! Caught you! The last time Gina sent her cousin from New York a letter was two years ago, before she let her hair grow. You've seen her all right!"

"So her hair is soft, is it?"

Luigi shot a look out the window at Red Rita, then stared down at the table.

"You see her and she tells you nothing. Gina. She leans against your cheek and lets you stroke her hair. Her eyes plead with you for help, her voice catches, and you cry. A grown man cries at what he does not know, at something he cannot understand, something he feels. And the pleading fades, and the words stop, and she removes her cheek from yours and she goes away. And you know nothing. Nothing. Every night I hear plenty, plenty in bed, believe me. Only Gina, quiet, wounded, beautiful Gina says nothing, asks nothing. I don't know what she wants. Mario adores her, but she is not happy. People talk. Some say it is because she has no children, but she wants no children. Others say it was because she was abandoned by a lover, but there was no lover. And still others say that her mind — that she is not herself, perhaps never will be again. But why?" Luigi shrugged.

"It must be hard on Mario."

"Very hard. If he whistles twenty girls come running. If he doesn't he gets only ten. Only Gina holds back, pulls away. I've seen it with my own eyes. I would not want to be Mario now."

"It was different when they got married," guessed Alan.

Luigi eyed him keenly for a moment. "Yes, it was different."

"She changed almost overnight."

Luigi was silent.

Alan hesitated. "Didn't she?"

Luigi stood up. "You ought to know, Cousin. Enjoy your breakfast."

The omelette was cold now, but Alan didn't care. He's double her age, he thought. Can't they understand that? Reason enough for her behavior. A good, older man who charmed a woman into a mistake she can't undo, can't explain. Have they no eyes to see? "The Old World is a strange world," he muttered. She had offered to be his servant for seven years before she claimed her freedom, as it says in the Bible. A servant in America. Alan shook his head. She

118

had wanted to die. He stared, half-seeing, at Red Rita's antics around the flower cart. "Gina is not mad. She has a reason for her behavior." He glanced at one of the faded murals of Rome before his eyes fell to the gold band on his finger. *As there is a reason for everything.*

Alan signaled to Luigi standing near the kitchen door, but Luigi merely waved. He made no motion to approach the table. Alan left a twenty dollar bill under the plate — generosity might prove helpful later — waved goodbye to his host, and hurried out the door. People thronged the walk, but Rita was gone.

Where was Gina? Luigi didn't know. Did Red Rita? Maybe Gina was in New York, maybe they had crossed oceans for each other in vain, the result of some senseless cosmic joke, but Alan dismissed that thought immediately. The air was too crisp, too active. He inhaled purpose. Had Red Rita met Gina's cousin in New York? Luigi did not know, could not understand, but a woman …Who have been the impassioned searchers into an understanding of "woman"? Have they not all been men? Perhaps women were not mysteries to one another. Red Rita … later. First, he would go shopping, shopping for women with information about Gina.

He would be her cousin from New York. Suddenly, he stopped. If she had a cousin in New York, why hadn't she prevailed upon that cousin to house her in that city? Perhaps Mr. Cousin's wife had prevailed. Perhaps he, Alan, really was her cousin. He tasted the air and threw back his shoulders.

The noises and smells of the day began to bear in upon him, striking glancing blows and bouncing off his alert, open senses, as he strode free, unencumbered of all but determination to find Gina. He had a mission. He vaguely wondered if he would be given enough time to complete it, and just as vaguely assumed that he would. He took off Mario's jacket, flung it over a shoulder, and walked — past fruit and vegetable vendors, past shawl vendors, past assorted shops that lined the street. He stopped at a leather shop and peered into the window. A woman smiled and motioned him to enter. He began to walk on.

"Mister, good leather, you come see." The woman stood outside the door of her shop.

Alan turned, uncertainty in his eyes.

"Come, come," she repeated, holding out a fleshy hand to him.

He walked back to where she stood and gazed at his reflection in the window. "I look like an American, don't I?"

The woman laughed. "Is good. I like Americans."

"I'm visiting my cousin Gina. Maybe you know her."

"What her last name?"

Alan stood for a moment, open-mouthed. An important oversight; he hadn't asked.

The woman laughed again. "My daughter Gina. You like to be her cousin is fine with me. Beautiful girl, my Gina. Big for her age. How you say —well-developed."

"How old is she?"

"Mmmm." The woman wagged her head from side to side. "What age you like?"

"Twenty-five, thin, with long, black hair, and a face more haunting, more beautiful than the Mona Lisa."

The woman shook her head. "You look for painting, not woman. Paintings not very good in bed. The shape is wrong. But they give you pleasant dreams. You like pleasant dreams? Come, you come into my shop you find something nice for when you find your Gina. Beautiful handbag or gloves. Come, look."

"Do you know any other Gina?"

The woman looked thoughtful. "Maybe yes. I must think. You come inside?"

Alan smiled weakly. "Maybe later."

The woman shrugged and Alan walked on. How many Ginas must there be in Venice?

A woman passed him, and the odor of provolone attacked him from the top of her shopping bag. He was sorry he had eaten. He felt the bills in his pocket — American money that would surely be accepted without question — and was sorry he had overpaid Luigi.

Bad judgment. In a pinch could he do nothing right? He continued walking. Suddenly he was in the midst of riotous colors and clashing odors. He began sampling the wares before him, sampling and talking, his American money causing slight stirs, slight arguments before acceptance, and an excuse for broken Italian conversation about "my cousin Gina, a stranger since her marriage." Everyone knew a Gina. There was Gina of the big bosom, Gina of the large hips, petite Gina, Gina of the arched brows. Alan mentioned Mario, to no avail. The list continued: Gina of the crooked nose, heavy Gina, thin Gina, tall Gina, Mama Gina! Alan felt himself getting sick — from ingestion of so much food and from the prolificacy of Ginas. Purpose was being suffocated by reality. He felt a firm grip on his right arm. He turned to face a thin, pinch-faced young man with unruly hair.

"You want Gina Monteleone," he said in a low, cracked, sure voice.

"Yes," said Alan, not knowing whether he did or not, and wondering at the youngster's good English.

The fat mistress of the shoe stalls frowned at them, and a warning voice shouted "Paulo!" as they elbowed away from the market color and sounds.

The young man leaned against the wall of a building facing the market. His eyes scanned the proceedings there as he spoke.

"Why you look for your cousin now?"

"I told you, I haven't seen her since her marriage."

"Four years a long time. Why you not come sooner?"

Alan threw his hands out in exasperation. "I just didn't."

The young man glared at him. "You're an American, all right. Now you want to be Italian again. Trouble at home, maybe? With a wife, eh? Now you want family."

Alan reddened. "Now I want family. Do you know where I can find Gina?"

"No one has seen her for two days. Think maybe she's finally left Mario. All talk."

121

"What do you think?"

"I think she's left Mario."

"For another man?"

Paulo shrugged.

"I have to find her. Have you any idea where she might be?"

Paulo considered this. "I have ideas," he said.

"I'll make it worth your while if you'll help me."

"For yourself or Mario?"

Alan was clearly amazed. "Why, I don't know! Maybe for neither. Maybe just for herself."

"Hmph," snorted Paulo. "You'll never be an Italian."

"Is it necessary?"

Paulo gave him a crooked smile. "No. You want to start now?"

"Yes."

"Okay." And he turned his back on the market and motioned Alan to follow.

From behind came shouts of "Paulo, Paulo," but the young man seemed not to hear. He set a leisurely pace past ships loading, gondolas pushing off into the blue-green waters, outdoor cafes coming alive, and people creating moving patterns along the water-lapped walk.

"I don't mind walking faster," suggested Alan.

Paulo gave him a sidelong look. "You see people walking faster?"

They continued in silence to the Piazza San Marco. Except for a generous sprinkling of pigeons underfoot, it was deserted, the tables and chairs empty.

"She came here every Tuesday morning to talk to a priest. She always sat here, facing the cathedral until he came to her."

"But she's gone! She won't come here now."

Paulo shrugged. "Maybe yes, maybe no. Today is Tuesday."

"She's run away. It's illogical to expect her to come back here."

"Logic has nothing to do with it. We talk of things of the heart. She will come back."

"What makes you so sure?"

"She has asked to see Father Bema again. She has never asked for the same priest twice."

Alan looked bewildered.

"You see," explained Paulo, "she has spoken to all the priests in Venice, each week a different one. Father Bema is the last, a very old man. Some say he has been dead for twenty years, but Gina asked to see him again today."

"Does Mario know this?"

"Only that today she sees a priest."

"But you know that it will be Father Bema."

"I know that."

"I don't think I would like to face Mario here."

Paulo smiled his crooked smile. "I don't blame you, but there is no place to hide in the Piazza. Still, you face the house of God, a comfort if you run fast."

Alan bristled. "I hardly think that will be necessary."

"Come." Paulo inclined his head toward the cathedral.

They entered, and Alan's nostrils breathed in the aroma of settled wood. He felt secure. "We stay here and wait for Gina?"

Paulo nodded. "Good. You understand."

Alan wasn't sure he understood in Paulo's terms. What he understood he could not clearly say, but a house of worship could be trusted. It exuded a confidence one expected from the living, not the dead, not from wood and stone and gold fashioned long ago, encumbered by the weight of centuries, rooted to a place that took no heed of time. Alan thought he would like Father Bema.

Paulo was silent, and it occurred to Alan to wonder why he had left the market where he worked and why he had chosen to help him when no one else would. But as he looked out into the Piazza framed by the doorway, his eyes glazing with the growing familiarity of the scene, it occurred to him to wonder why he was remembering a half hour spent in a small church in the French countryside. He and Jane had held hands, and the warmth of that had seemed to kindle a kindred warmth in their surroundings. The floor boards, like creaking knees, had kneeled with them. The pews, well-worn, their sharp edges long since rounded, had accepted them, strangers in time and place, and yet not strangers at all. The simple altar, lectern, and cross reflected ideas reborn, renewing links to the simplicity of an earlier time. Embellishments, thick and complex, could blot out the forms supporting most of life, but here was the simplicity of substance and warmth, of clarity and hope, not the chill of glass or the drama of buttresses flying. It was a warm simplicity, an old simplicity, an enduring one.

Alan's eyes adjusted to the cathedral walls. They wore elaborate carvings, deep and dark, illumined by a muted sparkle of color. This was no country church, but all around him Alan saw a captured complexity, a comprehensible complication. Simplicity after all.

His body felt stiff from the position he had held. He strained to read his watch in the dim light. "Two hours!" His voice attacked the walls.

"Shush," warned Paulo "Two hours is nothing in Venice. But perhaps you are right. Father Bema has left the Piazza. There is no point in waiting."

"Father Bema!" Alan almost shouted again "Why didn't you tell me!" He dragged Paulo into the striking sunshine of the now-crowded Square. "Where is he? Point him out to me!"

"He is gone. Gina did not come. Be calm, there is another way."

Alan ran out of the Piazza, nearly throwing Paulo off balance as he pulled him along. "Can you see him?" His anxious glance darted everywhere, looking for a white head, a frock, a collar, a he-knew-not-what.

"He is gone, I tell you." Paulo adjusted his collar. "I'm helping a madman!"

"I wanted to meet him."

"He does not know where Gina is or he would not have left."

"Still ..."

Paulo was impatient. "We are wasting time. You must find Gina, and I must go back to work. Father Bema cannot help us."

"For an old man he is fleet of foot," mourned Alan.

Paulo hid his puzzlement in anger. "You are more interested in the old man than in the girl!"

"He has seen a lot of foolishness in his time. He is old and wise." Alan raised questioning eyes to Paulo. "There is a Father Bema, isn't there?"

Paulo laughed more heartily than Alan would have thought possible. "Yes, there is a Father Bema. You would have seen him had you not been dreaming."

Alan nodded. "You said there is another way?"

"Yes. If Gina is hiding in Venice we can persuade her to come out."

"I hope she is still in Venice."

"She is. I am sure of that."

This was the first indication to Alan that Paulo had any interest other than a financial one in helping him find Gina.

"How can we persuade her?"

"Gina is a woman of mystery and drama with a weakness for beautiful clothes. You said at the market that you are in show business."

"Well, advertising, yes."

"Put on a show of beautiful clothes. It will be a magnet, and if we watch carefully, we will find Gina."

"You like Gina, don't you." It was a statement.

Paulo sighed. "Gina, the impossible one. How can one help but like Gina? But I would like her better if she went back to Mario and became a true wife to him."

"You are a fine friend to old Mario."

"That pig!" Paulo spat on the ground. "Straw and cornmeal would be too good for him. Make the show tonight. I will be there."

He walked off with no word of parting, but Alan did not notice. His mind was already working on a plan. This was no pleasure journey that he had undertaken or, perhaps more correctly, that had undertaken him. This was a mission of mercy, worthwhile, perhaps even vital. This was not merely work, but work it would require. For the space of a breath he registered amazement at his determination, but that space was succeeded by a certainty of the rightness of his decision. His lack of Italian would be no barrier, his lack of friends would be no barrier, his lack of any meaningful knowledge of Venice would be no barrier. He would create the biggest, the best, the most crowd-gathering, the most effective ad for a product in all Venice! A living ad, a la Red Rita, that would draw even that show-woman to his display, and maybe, yes, maybe Gina, too. A woman pulled her daughter back from the water's edge, as modest activity on a tug sent a brief spray into the air.

"That's it!" shouted Alan. He would introduce an all-weather dress! He had an almost tangible vision of Gina drenched, her dress clinging tenaciously to her body, the fabric making a brave, not altogether futile show of flare. He would seek out the smallest dress shop in the city. He would select clothes that looked appealing even when water-logged. He would find beautiful girls of all shapes and sizes to model them. He would hold a show of the dresses, wet and dry, on the dock. What a coup for the shop owner, what a triumph for himself, what a feast for the eyes of all Venice. He could barely contain his excitement as he entered the hotel. His hand went to his shirt pocket. American Express would see him through. He was sure of it; he willed it to be so. A warm bath later, Alan sat on the window seat in his room, his legs drawn up almost to his chin, and looked at the bustling life spread before him. But he looked only for a moment. In another time, another situation, he would not have drawn himself away with such alacrity, but he did so now. He skipped down the corridor steps and was out the front door before the doorman had finished bowing. He remembered a shopping area from five years past. How could he forget? One of Jane's fluffy pink creations and one of his favorites had come from a little shop there. Not that it mattered, of course, but it would be thrilling to select that very shop for the greatest ad campaign of his career. He walked more quickly. So what if his speed set him apart? He was an American, and he was in a hurry. Anyway, he was Gina's cousin, was he not? Let him stand apart in the eyes of Venice. He would be recognized for what he pretended to be. It would draw Gina to him. And when she saw the man she had begged to save her, she would not disappear into the alleys and byways of Venice. She would come forth and be saved. He wasn't sure exactly how, but wasn't that why he was in Venice? The answer would come. His hands swung vigorously at his sides and his eyes shone. In his creased pants, and open-necked, rumpled, white shirt he felt every inch a savior.

Louisa's was not quite the same as the shop of memory. Once chipped and faded, the sign looked freshly painted, but the name was reassuringly familiar. Once cluttered and pale, the window now glowed with colorful clothes neatly spaced and placed on view, but the dummies on which they hung looked old and worn. The past as bridge to the present. That was the way with beginnings. He entered the shop. An eager-faced, young woman hurried to his side. She was not Louisa.

"You are not Louisa," he said.

"Mama retired from the business two years ago," she responded in perfect English. "My Carlo and I, we have the shop now." A thin-faced young man emerged from the back room as if to underscore this fact. "You bought from Mama?"

"Gina did."

The young woman beamed. "Your wife, you wish to surprise her with something nice now."

Alan flushed. A mad impulse had shot through his brain and caused him to make this stupid, unthinking error.

The woman mistook his red cheeks for awkward acquiescence, and led him to a rack at the rear of the shop. "Very special. Copies from Paris." She fingered the fabrics with affection.

"Your wife takes a small size, yes?"

He said yes, and she was gratified to hear it. All the dresses were Parisian small.

"You don't understand," Alan blurted out. "I'm not here for my wife. I'm here to help you."

The woman took a step back, and said nothing.

The ad man in Alan took over and spoke.

Chapter Nine

SHE LOOKED DOWN AT THE smooth face couched in the pillow. The long lashes lay like a benediction on the milky skin. Wisps of black hair ventured onto the surface, but the face of the sleeping lady did not stir. The older woman sighed and shook her red head, red even in the semi-darkness of the room.

"So you've come back, dear child," she addressed the sleeping figure. "You are not lost to us. At least — " She bit her lip. "May heaven guide you." She made the sign of the cross and quietly left the room.

The young woman turned on her side, opened her eyes and sat up. Even in the darkness she knew the place. She exhaled deeply in relief, but even as she did so her face creased with concern. She had been close to freedom, to escape. This place, comforting as it was, was merely refuge. Another country, another life, a man who could help her find her way — this reality had retreated. Had it not been almost within her grasp, or had that merely been a dream, a hope so consuming that it had almost sprung to life through sheer will? Rita would be good, as always, and kind, and understanding, but she would have no answer. She could only care. But caring was not enough. Mario knew that too well. What more there could be she did not know. She had no doubt that God and Love were one, that to live love was all-important. I Corinthians 13 had through the years become a part of her. She loved and was loved, but she was not satisfied. Sacrilegious as it seemed, she was not satisfied. There had to be something else, something that would fill the emptiness inside her. She yearned for an answer, fearing that there was none. The bed creaked as she arose. She was meant to keep her appointment with Father Bema. She would do so. With the ease of experience she left the house unnoticed. The glare of daylight surprised her. She drew a long, ungainly shawl around her figure. Dull and rough, the material seemed to fall in folds around a shapeless body. The form thus enclosed could have been twenty or two hundred to anyone interested enough to conjecture the age of the woman hurrying to the Piazza San Marco.

The Piazza was crowded. She looked nervously around for Father Bema. People ate with relish or studied indifference at tables set for lunch. Waves of fragrance ebbed and flowed and followed her around the Square, but Father Bema was patron of none of them. Her mind whirled with the aromas, and she leaned against a chair to steady herself. It struck her that she had not eaten for a long while. Oh, where was Father Bema! She did not want to eat. She had no time to eat. She grasped the chair tightly. She must not faint! She eased herself onto the seat. The church bell chimed one o'clock. The sound sank through her body like a stone. One. "In the midst of life ..." One. Alone. Father Bema had come and gone. She had not been meant to see him today at all. She was too tired to think. Too hungry to dream. She crossed herself.

"Thy will be done," she said softly

"Aay? What was that?"

Gina looked at the bent old man, his hand cupped to his ear.

"I wasn't talking to you," she said.

"Should ha' been. You want to talk to yourself you go in there." He pointed to the cathedral. Gina looked away. The old man's shirt collar needed a turning, and she had no energy to argue. She would sit quietly for a few minutes to regain her strength for the long walk back to her friend's home. But the old man pulled up a chair facing hers and gazed intently into her face.

"Please go away," she murmured. "I'm only resting for a few minutes. I don't want to talk."

"Come here to eat or talk. Only Americans rest here, nothing surer. They are my hobby. I am the expert on San Marco Americans. Since my grandson's family moved me here with them from Verona I've had nothin' to do. The old men here, bah! They are a bore. I should have stayed with my old friends in Verona. Good talk, good jokes, good card games, good bocce. At least some green grass, somethin' solid under your feet. So I come here and watch Americans. From mornin' 'til night, Americans. Very interestin', amusin', profitable, too." He rubbed his hands together. "Not too many now, but soon it will be rainin' Americans. Rainin' Americans, do you understan'?" He chuckled at his words, then threw up his hands in disgust. "How do you get used to all this water?"

Gina smiled faintly. "How long have you been in Venice?"

"Three years."

"Wait another fifteen."

"Fifteen? I will go mad. But maybe not. I have my Americans."

"I wonder ..." She hesitated. "I wonder if you have seen mine."

"Italian born and you have lost an American husband?" He clicked his tongue in disapproval.

I did not think to watch Venetians. You left him in the Piazza?"

"He is a tall man," she said quickly, "with soft brown hair. He was wearing a white shirt and brown pants."

"And still is, no doubt. Or perhaps not?"

"Perhaps not," she conceded.

The old man rubbed his chin. "Crazy American hidin' in the cathedral little while ago. Had brown hair when he went in and when he came out. Draggin' one of the boys from the market. An American, all right." He grunted disapproval. "Shirtsleeves and brown pants. That your man?"

Gina creased her brows. "I don't know. You say he was dragging someone?"

"Thin kid with a beak nose from the market. My grandson Paulo."

Gina started.

"Dragged him to the street before he let go. Kept lookin' around for somebody. They talked and then split."

Gina looked alarmed. "They what?"

"They separated."

"I see." She twisted and retwisted the fringes of her shawl.

The old man signaled to the waiter. "The way I figure, you give him the slip and he's lookin' for you with a little native help. Now you're thinkin' you don't want to lose him."

The waiter set a steaming bowl of minestrone in front of her.

"Eat! You're about to faint dead away. Can't have any of that. That's right, that's right, put it away."

She looked puzzled.

"Means empty the bowl. And the bread, too. Good, ain't it?" He watched with satisfaction as she ate. "Your husband take you back you think?" he asked softly.

The spoon clattered into the nearly empty bowl. "What are you talking about?" she said almost harshly.

"Now, now," he continued softly, "no use gettin' huffy with me You're no more married to an American than I'm nine and twenty. Just askin' how the husband's takin' it. If there's no goin' back…"

"There's no going back because I won't go back, and thank you for the soup, but it's none of your business."

"You're very welcome, I'm sure, but not quite right. I've made Americans my business, and I'm thinkin' of startin' a follow-up on some of them after they leave the Piazza. Some involvement, ya know, to broaden my expertise. Thinkin' of startin' with the one hidin' in the cathedral. Think he'd be a good choice?"

"He's not my lover. I just want him to get me away. I'm so unhappy here!"

The old man nodded. "I'd rather be somewhere else myself."

"Then why don't you go?" She spoke accusingly.

"Where to? Ain't gonna be no different somewhere else, except in my dreams."

"Whatever the future holds can't be be worse than this eternal sameness, this unending boredom."

"You're a gambler," said the old man.

"I'm a realist."

"You're a romantic."

"I'm being practical."

The old man patted the table and smiled. "Maybe we're both right. Maybe it is realistic to take a chance. Maybe it *is* practical to be romantic." He pointed to the cathedral. "If you go in there they'll tell you that Jesus did not run away. He wasn't happy with the goin's on around him, but he stood his ground and, in time, his thought became the thoughts of most people. Spilled over into action a bit, too. Couldn't be helped. Irresistible ideas will do it every time, they say."

"And you think I can work wonders wherever I am?"

"Don't think anythin'. Only tellin' you what they'd probably say in there."

"Well, I'd rather work my wonders somewhere else."

"Do you see me stoppin' ya?"

"Do you think you'll see this American again?"

"Rarely see the same one twice. But if I do a follow-up, of course…"

"Will you?" she breathed.

"Don't know. Depends. Might be better to follow up someone else. I'm too old for complications and trouble. Watchin' Americans is only a hobby, ya know. Tryin' to enjoy my twilight years. Now if there were somethin' in it for me, maybe I would look up your friend."

"I have no money; I can't even pay you for the soup and bread."

The old man waved the thought away. "That's nothin', nothin', the soup and bread, I mean. But your young man…"

"Oh, I couldn't ask him! I couldn't!"

"He's gonna use money to help you, ain't he? To get you across the ocean, buy you clothes and stuff, ain't he?"

"That's different. But to ask him for the money itself—no!"

"Well, then, I can ask him."

"No, I won't have you do that; you mustn't do that. What a horrible thought!" She rose with energy, the result of her repast evident. Thank you for the soup. Goodbye."

He half rose as she hurried off. "I'm only an old man!" he called after her. "Just a poor old man." He sat down heavily. "Wants to be a modern woman and won't pay for the privilege. Got to pay to be free — and to be a slave and everythin' else, when it comes to that."

★★★★★

Alan ran the back of his hand across his brow. Interviewing women who were beautiful or who thought they were beautiful was sweaty business. He didn't know what to say — the same questions repeated over and over now sounded ridiculous to him — or where to look. Hips, breasts and behinds danced before his eyes. A breast bobbed near his chin, and all he could think of was Macbeth's "and be these juggling fiends no more believed that palter with us in a double sense" — and Jane. Jane did not play games. Jane was more than breasts and buttocks. She was — she was far away, an ocean away, ideas away. He nodded mechanically and waved from the window to Sophia guarding a line of girls on the dock. Eight girls would be enough. The interviews were over. He opened the window wider and looked beyond the gathering and street bustle below to the water traffic. Which clothes would look as good wet as dry? Sophia had already made the preliminary selection of clothes that would not self-destruct in the wash. She would model one as well, in honor of the matrons whose svelte figures were now but a memory. Alan ran his hand across his brow again. Choosing among women did not please him. He had never chosen a woman in his life. Both Elaine and Jane had been necessities, brought on by an inner compulsion that would not be cast aside. In business he had left such choices to Byron. He would leave the choice of clothes to Sophia. He thought of Gina. The urgency of Gina crossed his mind. His insides stirred. Hunger pangs. He ruefully remembered his supper date with Jane. He had never been late for a date with Jane, though he had waited often enough for her. But this last date was not with Jane. It was with Vanessa. Byron would be with Jane, partaking of Jane's company, and, if he could, of Jane herself. His eyes shot wildly to the water. If he dived in could he get back to New York in time?

With words and signs attending, Sophia was dismissing the girls below. Carlo stuck his head past the door.

"Signor Blaiser, a very good place to eat. You come, we talk clothes, yes?"

"Make it The Magic Pan," Alan said wistfully.

Carlo gave a cracked laugh. "Forest too far to go. We eat Luigi's."

★★★★★

Luigi's was crowded. Although the customers were seated and orderly, loud voices and gesticulations gave the impression of explosive activity. Luigi's was a veritable cross-section of Venice. Fisherman and shopkeepers, office workers of all sorts, and the well-to-do mingled like the aromas curling from the heated platters. Luigi himself seated them, as he did every other group or couple, undoubtedly one of the reasons for the place's success. One bite into the Luigi Venicia gave Alan another more compelling reason. Good food and a warm welcome; good clothes and attractive containers. A reasonable parallel. After each course Sophia and Carlo led him the round of the tables. Carlo stood awkwardly behind her while Sophia did the talking, the laughing, the cajoling, the coaxing, the pushing of Alan forward — in short, the business. Alan hoped he did not look as foolish as Carlo. He did not feel like the president of Blaiser & Son. He felt uncomfortable, like a little boy being shown off to the neighbors, with credit to Mama for making it all possible.

He wondered why a Sophia couldn't help Gina, why a Red Rita couldn't help Gina. He regretted the idea of the fashion show, of his delicious lunch at Luigi's. He felt very small. From ten tables away he saw Luigi cast a quick look at him. It was a look of disapproval.

During dessert details of the fashion show were discussed. Within the hour word would be spread by mouth and store sign in the major shops and markets in the city. Alan bent for the last morsel of his scrumptious dessert. When he looked up again he saw Luigi at the back of the restaurant talking to Red Rita. Where had she come from? The door was almost flush with the dark stained wall, but he saw it.

Sophia rose, Carlo rose, Alan rose. They rippled smiles and nods as they wound their way free of the smoky, spice-imprisoned air.

"Five o'clock, then; it is settled. Right from work the men come, from the kitchen the women. They go home arm in arm. Give them something to dream about over supper, through the night. And in the morning — Louisa's! And many mornings and afternoons to come too, aye, Signor Blaiser?" Sophia beamed.

"Five o'clock, then," repeated Alan. He watched them as they walked off, Sophia voluble, animated, Carlo silent, his thin arm around her ample waist. Alan walked around to the rear of the restaurant and peered through the kitchen window. There was much scurrying to and fro, much heat, much activity. He opened the door and slipped inside, where he helped himself to a clean, white apron and a tray and, head slightly bent, followed a waiter out the kitchen door. He swung abruptly to his right and through the door that led to the living quarters upstairs. He waited and listened, then gingerly made his way up the stairs. A face popped up before his eyes. A cry escaped from Alan's lips, stifled only by his simultaneous effort to grab the railing.

"I'm all right," he breathed heavily into the rotund face of Red Rita. "I'm all right," he echoed feebly to Gina. They helped him up the stairs, and he insisted on stumbling unaided to the bedroom where, unthinking, he sank onto a silk-clad chair. He attempted to get up.

"Sit, already!" Rita stood, arms akimbo. "What are you?"

"I—I—"

"We don't play games in this house, Mister American. I call my sons, there be nothing left of you. Now say, what are you?"

"He'a friend, Mama."

Rita turned to Gina in surprise. "You know this?"

"'This' is a man, madam," hissed Alan.

"A friend," murmured Gina.

Rita considered the matter: a friend, a man. She appeared to give grudging, qualified assent. "Stand up."

Alan stood up.

"Walk!" Alan walked. "You all right. Sit here." She pointed to a hard, high-backed chair. "You stay here. You talk. Be back five minutes. Find you both here. Capisce?"

For a long moment there was silence.

"You don't look at all like your mother."

"Gina is not my mother. My mother died soon after I was born."

"Yes," Alan said, wishing he knew more to say, knowing Byron would. "I've been searching all over for you." He felt miserable. The words were coming out all wrong.

Gina took his hand. It was clammy, but she didn't appear to notice. "You are a good man, like my Mario. You wonder why I leave one good man for another," she said dully. "I do not know."

"Perhaps you do not love him."

"I love him, I love him," she said with feeling, "but" — her voice was barely above a whisper that Alan strained to hear— "but I do not love him enough."

Alan leaned back into the hard, rounded dowels of the chair. "Who is to say what is enough? Perhaps there is never enough. You may want to love him more than you can. You may love him enough."

"It is enough for Mario. It is not enough for me."

"What is it you love about Mario?"

"I love his rippling muscles, his strength, his gentleness, his color, his aroma."

"What more do you want?"

"I want to be myself."

"What does that mean?"

"I want to be young, to have adventures, surprises, to discover talents I didn't know I have, to meet people who delight me, who are different from those I know, who can make my life richer, who understand my heart. Mario rules my life. I want to rule it."

"But he's good to you …."

"But I'm not free. Mario only knows his family way. He won't change it for me, maybe he can't. Wives do what they are supposed to do. They are a title, a precious title, but a title. They are not allowed to dream out loud, to live a dream, even for a little while. There is too much to do, too much tradition to carry through. He acts older than his years. I love the tradition, the support my macho darling offers me, but not if it costs me my life, my dreams, the adventure of being young."

"He loves you."

"And I love him. But that love will die as the years go by, is already dying. Our love will turn to hate, because we will not be satisfied. Not all people in love should marry. I cannot change and Mario cannot change. We are too —"

"—different. But cannot change or will not change?"

"It comes to the same thing."

"Does it?" Alan thought of Jane, of his flirting with Vanessa, of Gilbey's trade of marriage dissolution. The business of one's emotions was a terrible business to traffic in. Where did the heart, the soul, the spirit fit in? They came from another country, a wonderful country to live in, if only one could. Or was it if only one would?

"Mario was eating lunch when I left the house and jumped into the water. I was free! At least I thought I was. The waters carried me to you and then back again."

"It is not easy to escape when you carry the past with you. The sea has brought you back. Doesn't that tell you something."

"Only that I am being tested. Why should the sea accept me on my terms?"

"Don't be foolish. You are not one with the sea."

"How oddly you talk. How strange that the sea should have led me to you. A test, surely And yet you chose the sea, too, did you not? You chose to search for more. The sea is wise."

"I did not choose the sea. The sea chose me. This entire episode was an accident. And I'm not searching for anything. I've got what I want right here on terra firma."

Alan reddened. He had just lied three times.

"Nothing is an accident, and if you have all you want you have very limited vision."

Had there been room to recoil, Alan would have recoiled. He had been struck. The dreamer had limited vision! "You'll be all right here with Rita. She'll help you work things out in your life. You don't need me." He rose to go.

"I hurt you. I am sorry. Just like with my Mario. But I thought you would understand. Do not go away. I need you."

"For what?"

"For whatever reason we were destined to meet. You are my gift from the sea and maybe — maybe I am yours."

Alan opened his mouth to respond as Red Rita opened the door.

"Well?" she demanded. "What you decide to do?"

Gina said nothing.

"We haven't decided anything," offered Alan.

"In a few minutes I be out by flower cart and you decide nothing. You love Gina?"

"I — I don' know!" Alan was flabbergasted.

"Why you follow her here?"

"I — I don't know. She needed help."

"What help you offer?"

Alan's discomfort crept into his voice. "A test for Mario." Alan rose with determination.

"What?" spat Rita.

Alan felt his determination waver. He took a deep breath. "Business!" he proclaimed. "I'm conducting a fashion show for Louisa's Dress Shop."

"A fashion show! How beautiful the clothes?"

"That will depend on the eye with which they are seen, but Sophia has selected only Parisian designs."

"Humph," grunted Rita. "It's always distance and beauty."

"Oh, how I would love to wear such beautiful things," exclaimed Gina.

"And you can," responded Alan. "You can be another model to test the designs that will be in the show."

Gina evinced a childish delight, and the expression on the face of Red Rita softened.

"Sophia's got a boat for the rest of the day. You change here, take a dip in the sea, and we'll see how you look."

The two women stared at him.

"Oh, I guess I haven't made the whole thing clear."

"You have made it very clear, skin clear," rumbled Rita ominously.

"No, no I haven't. You see, the clothes will actually be modeled that way, in front of a crowd, a very large crowd, we hope, to emphasize the beauty of the clothes by showing that they look good wet or dry. This will be a test for Mario. If he allows her this freedom, accepts it, he will allow her more. She is young! It should work, and it's a cute idea."

"Adorable," snapped Rita, "but not for our Gina."

"No, Mama. It is a good idea. It will not change Mario's mind. It is too set on tradition, but it will make him realize that he must let me go, that it is best for both of us. I will feel better about leaving him then. I can be free, free to find myself, to be myself in a new land with fewer traditions. I can go off to America with this young man — what is your name? — and discover what it means to be happy, at last!"

"You don't know his name?" Rita was aghast.

"Sophia has good taste, and all those beautiful clothes! Mama, I will make a statement, and Mario will see and understand and let me go."

"No one can keep you bambina, if you want to leave."

"I feel Mario pulling me toward him. I flee and the waters wash me back. He must not want me anymore. H will not want me after tomorrow night."

"Foolish talk, foolish talk," said Rita, clearly worried.

★★★★★

Alan breathed deeply as he walked toward the boat. Smells of the sea hung in the air, festooned with the shouts of the seamen and the cries that frame the routine of daily life. If his ears did not pick out the words, if his eyes saw only the activity and not the cause, he could echo Gina's spirit, hear the call she heard, and cast off to adventure! He would inhabit that fabulous painting, "A Pilgrimage to Cythera," and take a journey to an island of love, joy, and contentment. Why had he told Gina there was no escape, that she should return to Mario? Why had he spoken like an old man? His right knee gave under him, and he stumbled against a cart of apples and sent them flying. There were angry shouts and arm-waving. Alan quickly bounded for the fleeing apples. Oh, Watteau Watteau! This was his adventure, not a pilgrimage, not a journey to fulfillment, to love, but a reality where things fall apart. But the apples were now back in the cart, and this was now reality. Yet reality was far away, wasn't it? Reality was in New York with a wife who had no time for his silly dreams. He hurried on. "A Pilgrimage to Cythera" — from Cythera, some experts said — from Cythera. Were the voyagers leaving the very environment they yearned for? Were they leaving what their hearts and souls desired? His romantically formal Jane, so into artistic geometry, he wondered if Jane knew.

The tugboat lay as it had the day before, its faded bulk fitted snugly into its accustomed slot on the pier. Sophia had insisted on a tug — elegant clothes for the working class had been her theme — and of all tugs she had to choose this! Only the lowered plank indicated a possible welcome. As he set foot on the deck Alan saw the tug's owner, Mario. The muscles of his mouth worked slowly on the pipestem between his teeth.

"This time it's business," said Alan encouragingly. "I'm Alan Blaiser." He extended his hand.

Mario ignored it, got up and walked to the quarters the models would occupy. Alan followed.

"You seea the place before, you seea again. Okay?"

"Okay. A little cramped, but all right for a changing room." He hesitated. "Sophia paid you?"

Mario nodded. "Mario no be here for show. Something go wrong, den something go wrong. Your problem. You damage boat Mario break you to pieces or you pay, your choice."

Alan made an unsuccessful attempt to laugh. "I guess you don't much like me. Can't say I blame you."

"Dun know you, dun wanna know you. Godda problems enougha my own."

"Yes, yes, I know — Gina."

"Bigga mouths all over island."

"May I ask how long you've been married?"

"Why? You wanna marry my wife? She dead. Ina the grave. You still interested?"

Alan laughed nervously and turned to go. Suddenly, muscular hands grabbed him by the throat. Their grip tightened.

"Where Gina? You tell me now!" Mario released his hold and hurled Alan to the wall.

Alan massaged his throat and saw a tiger ready to spring again.

"What if I say I don't know," croaked Alan, his eyes on the exit.

"Den you crazy, you lie, you talk just like Gina. You tell me or —"

"So she's crazy, too?" asked Alan, stalling.

"Only stranger crazy. Gina, she has dreams."

"If she wants to go, will you let her go for good?"

"No good for Gina to go. No good for anyone. But if she knowa for sure she wanna go, den Mario — maybe. Maybe. Is hard to led go. Very hard. If she knowa for sure ..." The thought seemed to weaken him. His body sagged, and he collapsed in a chair.

His weakness strengthened Alan. "She'll be here in an hour. She's in the fashion show. I suppose you've heard about it."

"Naked!" Mario's eyes bulged.

"No, no. She'll be modeling wet clothes, dry, then wet. A publicity idea."

Mario shook his head. "Isa de same. For sure she wanna go. Bud why she nod stay away? Why nod ride ledder, like in movies? Why disgrace Mario?"

"She wants to make a statement, a final statement. She's set on doing it."

Mario slumped in his seat. "Den her love for Mario dead, dead for sure."

"I — don't think so," Alan ventured. "It's all right if we're here in an hour, then?"

There was no response.

"It's been paid for. Word is out all over Venice."

Again, there was no response.

"It's good publicity for your business."

Mario turned glazed eyes on Alan.

Where did truth end and interference begin?

"She does love you, though. She told me so."

Mario sat silent, unmoving. Alan quietly left the room.

Young boys staunchly guarded the speakers spaced around the fringes of the waterfront, which was now thick with people. A hundred yards beyond the gangplank men with binoculars laughed, joked, and jostled one another. A curious expectancy filled the crowd, or perhaps it was merely an expectant curiosity. Alan could not tell as he struggled to separate the emotional from the business aspects of the enterprise. He could not pick out Mario in the crowd. He had apparently kept his word and stayed away, but the rest of working Venice had come. Old and young, male and female they had come — to see Parisian fashion, to see youth, to see female beauty. He hurried aboard the boat, passing Sophia, wireless microphone in hand, on her way to the gangplank to introduce the show.

"Everything ready. Girls ready to go." Her voice was firm and clear. Only the paper shook slightly in her hands.

Alan took up his position outside the cabin door. Upon demand he would unsnag a zipper, give the girls their cues, inform Sophia if the next model was not ready. He felt nervous, despite the ambivalent feeling that this was and was not his show. The cues began, and so did Alan's thoughts.

"Marie!" MARIO COULD NOT ENDURE THE SHAME. HE WOULD NOT TAKE HER BACK.

"Carlotta! " GINA WOULD BE FREE TO GO WHERE SHE WISHED, FOR STARTERS WITH HIM. BUT WHAT WOULD HE DO WITH HER? HOW WOULD HE PREPARE HER TO BE ON HER OWN, TO BE INDEPENDENT, FREE?

"Suzanna!" SHE WOULD BE LONELY AND WOULD NOT FORGET. SHE WOULD MISS THE OLD SIGHTS AND SOUNDS, THE SECURITY THEY OFFERED. SHE WOULD MISS MARIO.

"Concetta!" AND MAYBE NOT. HER VISION WAS CLEAR. GINA WOULD SUCCEED. SHE WOULD BE HAPPY EVEN IF OTHERS WERE NOT, EVEN IF STREWN IN THE PATH OF HER CLIMB TO SELF-FULFILLMENT LAY THE ANGUISHED HEARTS AND SOULS OF THOSE WHO LOVE HER.

"Gina!" I COULDN'T BE HAPPY LIKE THAT.

Gina emerged from the cabin. Around her head there seemed to shine a halo, casting a warm light, a softness, a purity on the features of her determined face, on the sleeveless black crepe dress dipped low in the front and barely existent in the back. She passed him with a radiant, almost unseeing glance, With stereo crispness he heard the shouts. Had there been shouts for the girls who had gone before? Disturbing, banned-in-Boston shouts. This, then, was success. But there was something more and something less. More shouts than seemed appropriate, less from Sophia. No patter of descriptive monologue, no "Carla! Juliana! Rena!"

Alan ran onto the deck. Like a high priestess from the land of myths, Gina stood cornered on a box to the side of the ramp, the wet, floor-length crepe molded to her body, her feet, for all anyone could tell, a vertical, well-balanced set of fins, her long, straight hair shining wet. It was a regal pose. Only her eyes reflected a muted fear. At the base of her pedestal, surrounded as by a laurel wreath, four men fought. As one fell, he was replaced by another. Like a game of "tap" the fighting cut a path through the crowd, spreading vertically, horizontally, diagonally. It occurred to Alan that Jane would enjoy the symmetry of it. But what of the human emotions, what of the very real Gina atop the box? Sophia waved to him from her retreat at the other end of the boat. It was not a wave of joy. The back of the dock was now a phalanx of women, though many fought and screamed their way close enough to the cause of the melee to prompt the goddess to assume a more erect stance and strike a more courageous pose. Alan's stomach informed him that he had made another mistake. At leisure he would calculate its magnitude. Before he felt entitled to that luxury he would have to rescue Gina. As he scanned the sky for help from above he saw the rope swinging from the smokestack. He did not want to shinny up that stack to grab hold of it; he did not know how to shinny up that stack. He looked around. A huge straw-topped crate on wheels sat unobtrusively to his right. He got behind it, put his shoulders to it, and sent it rolling to the key group of fighters stage left. Shouts of warning preceded the cart. The players turned in earnest on Alan. He climbed the smokestack in seconds, pausing only long enough to contain his astonishment at his feat, and to note that one of the men was on his way up to him. He grabbed the rope and swung out over the tug, catching Gina about the waist, as he dropped the rope and flew with her through the air into the darkening water.

"Put that on your canvas if you dare, Jane Blaiser!" thought Alan as he struck the water. The water created a storm of its own in his head, and the one on shore appropriately faded. He and Gina swam to Venetian soil ahead. Alan hoped that when they reached it they would find they were pulling themselves up onto the New York City waterfront, but it was not to be. Had there been a moon, it would have illumined the features of two drawn-faced people who clung to each other. There was a rush of water behind them. A thin man emerged from the water almost on the run, which he continued as he moved ahead of them, motioning them to follow. A glance back at the water, alive now with swimmers, convinced them to do so. The poorly lit streets would have filled Alan with foreboding had he had the time to think about them. As it was, whisking up and down them merely made him uneasy. With Gina's hand in his he ran. Their leader led them to a modest-looking house, which even the waning daylight revealed to be in obvious need of a coat of paint. The door opened without any of them breaking stride. They collapsed in chairs immediately.

"Foolishness didn't work out, eh?" The old man from the Piazza put down his binoculars. Gina started.

Alan looked wary.

The thin man bolted upright. He was Paulo. "We need your help, Grandpa."

"Likely, likely," the old man said. He turned to Gina. "Found your 'husband' I see. Gonna live happily ever after in my house?"

Gina stiffened and rose. ·

"If so, gonna have the devil of a time doin' it. Ain't got no house. This here's the gift of my grandson. His, really. Hard to say no to Paulo. Offered to help you once, anyway."

"You met her and you said nothing to me about it?" Paulo asked his grandfather.

"Didn't know who she was. Just a pretty young woman in trouble, seemed to me." He turned to Gina. "Don't recall your offerin' your name to me, young lady. That's not a reprimand, mind you. Mystery is good for the spirit. Your man here has found you to take you away from this dreary life, and Paulo has found you to —"

"Grandpa, no more! I must leave now. Half the men of Venice will be here soon. When they come do not suddenly become the good neighbor."

"Certainly not! That would be highly suspicious."

Paulo grasped the old man's hands. He bent low as if to kiss him on the cheek. "Say nothing," he whispered, and fled the house.

"Hungry, thirsty, sleepy? What is your pleasure?"

"Nothing, thank you. Mario will kill me if he finds me, but that will be freedom, too."

"Don't talk like that," rasped Alan "You will get your freedom."

"Let her talk. It costs nothin'. You keep talkin' too. Sounds good. From some American pitcher, ain't it? If you won't eat, drink, or sleep, nothin' much else to do, is there?"

"We can be silent," said Alan with dignity.

"Not healthy, not healthy at all. More trouble caused by people keepin' silent that anythin' else. But if talk don't interest you, you could get your damn behinds offa my chairs and into somethin' dry. That'll do for starters."

"No starda whad you canna finish." A man completed heaving his ancient bulk through the window. He glowered at Gina and Alan. "Shame, shame! And you." He lifted the old man's binoculars. "You! Go back to Verona, you and Paulo. You make filth in Venice!"

The two old men hurled themselves at each other. Gina muffled a scream. Alan was too surprised to utter anything.

Old Verona laid a right to the jaw of Old Venice. Old Venice, stunned for a moment, connected with a right hook. Alan's eyes moved in unison with the punches. A feint to the stomach and a slam to the floor, a side-stepped blow to the cheek, and a 1,2,3 punch to the face. A dance, a smash, a clinch.

147

Alan opened his mouth to shout them apart, but their names eluded him. They were merely two old men fighting. He turned to Gina. She watched the fight with fascinated horror. Gina, Gina and her —

"Mario! Mario!" shouted Alan.

His name threw Old Venice off guard for a moment, enough for Old Verona to knock him to the floor. A hurried survey of the room assured the downed man that Alan should be his next target. He wobbled to his feet, bent his head low, and began a running ram–like attack.

"No!" shouted Gina, as she tried to step between them. Inadvertently smacked aside she achieved her aim. The men were all concern, even while berating her for her interference.

"Gina, Gina," heavily breathed old Mario, Old Venice of the swollen cheek. "Stay wid Mario. Mario love you."

"You do no such thing," finger-wagged Old Verona of the cut upper lip. "You do what my Paulo says, that's what you do."

"To break upa home? To kill the olda ways, de olda happiness?"

"That's what Paulo thinks best. My olda home broke up, my olda ways and my happiness."

"And whadda you godd now?"

"Probably a black eye, but I see what you mean. Still, I owe Paulo something."

"Paulo wants Gina to return to Mario," insisted Alan.

"After shaming his best friend?" Old Verona was astonished.

There was a knock on the door. Old Verona sidled to the window.

"It's Paulo. Now we will know what to do."

Old Venice bowed. "Welcome to the savior. Wadda we do now, your highness?"

Paulo cast a swift glance around the room. "They haven't come. It's only you, then."

"Only me. Nobody impordan. Jusd old Mario."

Paulo ignored him and walked to Gina. His voice was barely audible and it shook. "Go back to my friend Mario. Go back. You are all he sees."

"Bouda time you say so. Wasa your wife alwaysa runnin' after Mario. Mario only sees Gina. Isa de truth."

Paulo feigned unawareness of his words. "Gina, go back to Mario," he pleaded.

"He didn't come to see me in the show," she said dully. "He was ashamed."

"No, no," interrupted Alan. "You're missing the point. You want a new life. You want to be free!"

"No canna be free here, no canna be free anywhere," muttered Old Venice.

Even Alan ignored him. "You've got to leave, Gina. Come back when you're free, if you wish. If you stay now you will be chaining yourself to the past. Don't allow them to persuade you. You know you want to leave. Don't let Mario persuade you. Open your eyes! Can't you see he's an old man?"

A rock seemed to barrel into Alan's stomach. He was slammed into the wall and slumped to a halt.

"No talk abouda Mario thada way."

"Is this what you want?" croaked Alan. "Force?"

"Nobody force Gina, nobody."

Gina said nothing. Her face was a marble mask.

"Is this what you want?" Alan repeated.

Gina turned away.

"She no wanna talk, dadsa whadda she wan. Talk abouda force!"

Suddenly, the tugboat's brawny young man with jet black hair and a plaid shirt stood in the doorway.

"Mario!" said the old man, "My boy, my Mario!"

The newcomer said nothing. He did not seem to see the bruised faces of the old men or the presence of Alan or Paulo. He looked only at Gina and she unmoving and seemingly unmoved, looked at him. And so they stood.

"The earth stands still sometimes
      and holds its breath and waits,
And we wait with it — wait for action
      to come out from under our hands,
As we stand apart and watch,
As we stand still, too."

The young man stirred and walked slowly but resolutely toward the young woman. His lips separated, as if for speech, but no words came. And still she stood. It seemed a long time, but of course it was not, before Gina clasped the young man's hands in hers.

Alan shook his head in disbelief. "Gina, no," he breathed mechanically, but he felt his convictions crumble before the virile stranger. They had been built on a hoary head — and water. Gina made no sign of hearing. It suddenly struck Alan that the others had heard only what they wished, that he had heard only what he wished, too. Unbidden and unwelcome came Yeats' poem "The Cap and the Bells." Involuntarily Alan shivered. Gina had not wanted her own freedom at all. She had wanted young Mario's, the jester's cap and bells, his reason for being, his identity, his soul. And she had gotten them.

Old Mario was crying softly, his bruises glistening.

Paulo gave Old Verona a bear hug, as Alan wandered witlessly to the door. The purpose had gone out of his life. He couldn't get his thoughts to focus. He knew only that he didn't belong here. The night air was cool and damp. He walked down the steps and looked at the pinpoints of light in the blackness. A mocking voice snapped at him from behind.

"Hey, cousin-husband!"

Alan saw a bundle flying at him through the darkness. His hands opened reflexively to receive it. He caught it, stumbled, and fell with it to the ground.

"Always stumbling, always clumsy," he muttered angrily, as he lifted himself up on his hands and drew the bundled pea jacket along with him.

"You hurt, mister?"

Alan looked into the face of a boy of maybe ten, sandy-haired, eager-eyed, concerned.

"No, no, I'm fine. Just looking for something I lost, that's all." He saw the sun rising overhead. "Up a bit early, aren't you son?"

"Walking with my mom and dad," the boy said proudly. "Dawn is beautiful from this beach, just like my dad said."

Alan looked over his shoulder. "Morning tide. Do you come here often?"

"Oh, no! It takes us six hours to drive here from New York City."

Alan made some futile calculations as to their whereabouts. "Going back soon?"

"This afternoon, I'm afraid. Dad's got to get back to work tomorrow."

Approaching them from a distance were a man and woman holding hands.

"Think your parents might give me a lift back to the city?"

The boy's brow furrowed. "Well, maybe, but Mom's not too keen on strangers. Did you find what you were looking for?"

"Yes."

"What was it?"

"The way home, son."

"But you haven't got there yet," said the boy practically.

"No," said Alan, clutching Old Mario's pea jacket, "not yet."

Chapter Ten

JANE BLAISER PRESSED A BUTTON on her desk.

"Angie, Trumbull's on his way down to see how he's hung. Cancel Cartwright. I'm not up to staying late today. Any calls?"

"*Flower Children* called about an interview."

"Another one? Any other calls?"

"I'm sorry, Mrs. Blaiser, really sorry. Maybe — maybe he's got amnesia. It's possible."

Jane buzzed off without a response. Three days ago Alan Blaiser had washed himself out of her life. Small satisfaction that he had stood up Vanessa, not her. Small satisfaction that Byron had cleverly arranged a tête à tête, that he wanted her to be exclusively his. With the dim lights and the roar of the rain outside he could not have seen seen how pale she must have looked or given any special meaning to her laconic responses or her weak voice. Perhaps he had, and thought it all a romantic result of his magnetic charm. Alan would have done much the same thing and responded much the same way. Once. But Byron was a poor substitute for Alan. She tried to think why.

The magazine interview was probably ready for her examination. She removed the receiver from its cradle and dialed.

"Vanessa, please. Just Vanessa, one of your reporters. Yes, I'll wait." She looked out the window. An unpleasant image of several days past caused her to turn away. "What? What do you mean? Of course she exists. She interviewed me for your magazine. Connect me with the editor-in-chief. Jane Blaiser. Please do that. Until five. Yes. Thank you."

No Vanessa, no Alan. Was Byron a planned diversion? How she wished she could disappear too. Then she realized that she had. She fingered the button on her desk again.

"Angie, get me Matt Johnson, will you?"

"Oh, Mrs. Blaiser, not another Trumbull snag!"

"No, Angie. I'm getting a divorce."

★★★★★

The phone rang eight times before Alan got the front door open and zipped through the hall to the gossip bench.

"Yes?" he puffed into the receiver.

"Alan! You're not supposed to be there! Vanish! Begone! How can Jane plead desertion with you lounging around the house, probably with your dirty shoes on her best upholstered pieces? I'll add that to the charges too, if you don't leave immediately. What are you doing there anyway?"

"Gilbey! Go back to the Coast, buster. There's no money in this for you. I'm not leaving Jane."

"Mere semantics, dear boy. She's leaving you."

"For whom? Byron? That Bunny character?"

"I am not privy to that information and wouldn't tell you even if I were. Actually, Alan, Matt Johnson is unable to take the case, and having just been visited by this acclaimed divorce attorney who went through fifth grade with him, he asked me to contact Jane about handling it.

Since she threw me out of the apartment when last we met, I'm taking the precaution of offering my services via this instrument. Armed with Johnson's recommendation, my status as your former friend, and my not inconsiderable charm, I thought I would be successful. You intend to stay, then?"

154

"Yes."

"Ah, well," he sighed, "then I had better get my portly self to your abode and offer my services in person. Jane has already left the office. Perhaps she and I will arrive together, a fitting duo proceeding against the detestable Alan, who has proven unworthy of his faithful Jane."

"You're forgetting the Frick."

"I'm forgetting nothing, as my fee will reflect. You may expect me in fifteen minutes."

"Gilbey, you rotten — Gilbey! Gilbey!"

Alan put down the receiver and walked to the living room, to the bedroom, to the den — walked nervously through the apartment over and over again until he heard the key in the lock.

Jane entered, looked harried, windblown and beautiful.

Emotion choked him, but he managed a casual "Hi! I don't want a divorce."

Jane's surprise flashed quickly across her face. She moved toward the kitchen, Alan behind her.

"We're a hopeless couple," she addressed the air.

"We've been all right for six years."

"We've never been all right, and the more years we spend together the less right it becomes. We'll keep hurting each other because we don't meet each other's needs. We're too different, Alan. Let's be realistic and face it." She became absorbed in washing the lettuce.

"I can forgive the Frick business."

"There will always be something. I've made up my mind."

Alan was silent for a moment. "Matt Johnson can't take the case. He's asked Gilbey to contact you. The turncoat's just phoned. He'll be over in a few minutes. I'd rather not be here when he arrives. I might do something to prejudice my case."

"I don't relish being here, either. He's a detestable man."

"That's what he said I was, the detestable Alan."

Jane swallowed hard. When she spoke her voice was calm. "Not detestable, never that. Just mistaken, like me. We are a couple of mistakes."

"So we do have something in common. And we both hate Gilbey. Let's have dinner out, Jane. Some nice, quiet place. I won't press my case, honestly. Let Gilbey wait for his rejection."

"All right." Her voice had taken on its business edge. "Shall we leave a key for him under the mat?"

"It's more than he deserves but we will be kind."

Alan put a key under the mat, daring only to lead Jane by the elbow out of the building and to the car.

"I don't seem to have my car key, Jane. Let me have yours."

"Alan, you've got our house key. You must have put the car key under the mat."

"Well, so I did. Gilbey should have an interesting time toying with it." He revved up the motor and pulled away from the curb.

Alan stopped for a light "Did you have dinner with Byron that night?"

"Of course. I keep my appointments"

"I would have come if I could."

"I'm sure."

"Wouldn't you like to know why I couldn't?

"No."

"Wasn't Vanessa curious?"

"Really, Alan, this little game is beneath you. Pull in at Burger King; I don't want you spending my settlement money for me."

"You're being cruel again, Jane. Can't you be civil even now?"

"I'm being what? You ooh and aah me for six years, force me into dinner with romantic schlock, run off with another woman, and you tell me I'm being cruel and uncivil?"

"I meant every ooh and aah," said Alan with vehemence, "and what did I get in return? 'I've got to work late tonight Alan, business beckons from Dallas, Alan, sorry I missed you at breakfast, Alan.' For putting up with six years of that I should get a medal!"

"So I'm giving you a divorce; what more do you want, my soul?" She looked away. "You're holding up traffic."

The blare of horns suddenly entered Alan's ken. He lifted his stare from Jane and his thoughts from Gina and continued down the street.

"I didn't run off with Vanessa. If she's gone, she's run off with herself."

"As we have done," responded Jane, and Alan could only nod. "But we're not about to change," she added softly, "and there's the end to it."

There was silence between them as Alan drove past Burger King and pulled into Nino's parking lot. He went around the car to open the door for Jane. Silence as they followed the waiter to a table for two in the dimly lit room, as the waiter pulled out the chair for Jane, as they seated themselves.

The waiter returned with the menu, and Jane pointed to the items she was ordering.

After her last utterance there could be no more; she did not trust her voice. Alan concentrated conspicuously on the menu, then indicated his choices. The waiter went away.

Alan looked to his right, to his left. He looked over Jane's right shoulder and over Jane's left shoulder. He did not know what Jane was doing. He could not look at Jane.

The waiter was gone for years.

Jane looked at her nails, at the plates, at the silver. She was sorry that the menu head been taken away.

Dinner had been a very bad idea.

What had Old Verona said? That silence wasn't healthy? Alan remembered when it was. They would sit together in the den, he and Jane, each occupied with a different concern — a Marco Polo and a Norah Lofts, an especially mean crossword puzzle and the stamps of Mauritania. Or the setting was a cove on the Algarve in early morning, all sea and sand, and two very quiet people. Silence had been beautiful then. Now it was merely safe. Old Verona was old, but not wise. He had forgotten happiness and love. He remembered loyalty, but it was not the same. Old Venice understood love, understood at least his son's heart. He was the protector of love, not in words but in deeds. Alan swallowed hard. He sneaked a peak at Jane. But there is no way to net love. Love is its own net, its own protection against hate, disillusion, and challenge. Old Venice was not wise either. When Gina had disgraced him Mario had been absent, a form of silence. Yet he had come to her who had run off with a stranger, come to her and said nothing. And his presence and his silence had spoken.

Jane was looking at a candle-lit table across the room. In some vague way she found the distant light agreeable. The two people facing each other across it merely put the light in focus; they anchored the light. It cast prisms on the wall, like a finely cut diamond faceted, glowing, growing in depth and brilliance, dividing and looking back at her as the eyes of Baron Kisonauf. The dear Baron, looking out at her from the circle of two strangers' love, trapped in his own fire, his own bright blaze — and ignored. Her art had turned him into a rag, and he hadn't minded. To find redemption in whatever shape, he hadn't minded. And as a rag he had remained — no eye-blinding shine, no god-like form, no love. Baron Kisonauf! He had begged for her help, and she had tried. Foolish Baron! How he had pounced upon her, eager with hope. Why had he not pounced upon one of his clichés, upon "the blind leading the blind," upon the hopelessness of it all. Opposite her sat Alan, aglow with good intentions and actions that spoke the impossibility of their ever being realized. In the shadows lurked Vanessa, Ann Weller, and who knew how many more. Alan had a yen for romance, just as the Baron had had a yen for conquests.Venus had known the real Baron, just as she knew the real Alan. A slight smile escaped her lips, withdrawn only when she heard the movement of Alan's chair. Imagine, equating her knowledge with that of Venus! Taurus-born she was, but not from the sea.

Alan stirred and cleared his throat. He had seen the smile. What was Jane thinking? Perhaps of the moment they had met, when her obvious self-sufficiency, her calm beauty had won him instantly. How they had danced at Elaine's ball. They danced that way occasionally still. Or was she thinking of the time they had escaped the Gala bore of the year by climbing out a first floor window and getting his pants and her gown caught in the limb of a tree, from which only a generous assortment of guests armed with knives, hooks, advice, and encouragement could free them. Or it may have been the Algarve, or those quiet moments on the weekend when they awoke. It may have been any one of a dozen things they had made happen, but he hoped it was one of the quiet moments, one of the quiet pleasures they had shared in their six years together.

The waiter returned. He apologized profusely. How could he have forgotten to light their candle? No drinks, no soup, were they sure? They nodded their certainty. He served their entrees.

Alan blinked at Jane across the candle. She returned his gaze briefly, then turned her attention to the food. She felt his eyes on her as she buttered her bread, as she sliced her steak, as she lifted the carrots to her mouth. She looked up abruptly.

Alan was cutting his lamb. He had felt Jane's gaze on him from his first glass of water to his current forkful of split peas. He looked up sharply. Her eyes were fastened sullenly on the tablecloth. He put down his knife and fork and waited for her to look across the candlelight at him. It seemed a long while before she did, but he did not mind waiting. This was not the business Jane, or the kitchen Jane or the bedroom Jane. This was not the Jane who had enough time for him. But this was the Jane who was holding still long enough for him to recognize the Jane he loved.

When she looked at him her eyes were shining, glistening. Alan cupped his fingers around the flame. They sat that way until the waiter returned. Alan put his burnt fingers around the arm of the waiter as he attempted to relight the candle. Perhaps the gentleman did not understand: Nino's means romance.

"We're beyond romance," said Alan, breaking his silence.

"Liar!" Jane barely hid a laugh.

"Liar!" Alan hurled back happily.

Suddenly the weather became very important — skiing conditions, although neither skied, the possibility of another earthquake in Alaska, which they had no intention of visiting, the shortness of spring. The potted flowers sitting table center presaged the blooms that would grace window sills, sidewalks and street stands around the city, indeed, already had. Alan recalled his futile office gift to Jane just days before. He plucked a crocus for Jane, roots and all, thumbing a dollar bill into its place in the soil and placing a hundred dollar bill on the table for the meal. Neither took account of a voice shouting behind them. They descended the steps to the parking lot and the car. It was back to their apartment to face Gilbey, and then — ? Alan stopped for a light. A taxi pulled alongside his car and ground to a halt. A wildly gesticulating waiter jumped from the vehicle and began banging on Alan's window. A shouting match ensued. It stopped abruptly when Alan saw Vanessa.

"It's Vanessa!" he exclaimed to Jane.

"So?"

"So she hasn't run off!"

"Does that make you happy?"

"Of course not, but yes; she can explain everything."

"What everything?"

"Nothing! She can explain that everything is nothing. We mustn't let her get away! Get out your door and bring her in here."

"I will not! There's a raving lunatic out there! And she's a fraud; she's not a reporter."

"I forgot she was a reporter."

"I said she's not! You're the most stupid man I've ever met!"

"Stupid? Yes, to let you walk all over me for six years."

"You dare to say that? You've had more freedom in six years than most men would get in a lifetime!"

"You admit it! You've walked all over me with your freedom. Instead of devotion and attention I got freedom."

"I gave you plenty of devotion and attention — in concentrated doses! Any other man would cherish a wife like me. Byron —"

"Byron loves Ann, so stop dreaming!"

"Dreaming? You're the one who's dreaming. If I had known six years ago —"

Vanessa strode around the taxi, pad and pencil in hand. Trotting after her was her plump son. The street was narrow, and the taxicab and Alan's car made it impassible. There was a deafening din of horns. The taxi driver clapped his hands over his ears.

"Oh, Mother," begged Bunny, "can't we get out of here?"

"No, dear," responded Vanessa, "not yet."

An irate man emerged from another taxi, a woman tugging at his sleeve.

"George, come back and wait like everyone else."

"Oh, no! I'm getting you to a lawyer first. You're filing those divorce papers first. Your husband can go to hell with his. With me, you're first!"

A siren announced the arrival of the police. A uniform threaded its way among the cars to the cause of the congestion.

Alan and Jane took that moment to look beyond their glass enclosure. They met the belligerent gazes of Sergeant Weller, Adele, George and the waiter. Beyond them, a portly figure lay stretched, face down, across the front of the taxi "Bunny!" shrieked Jane.

Alan and Jane joined the others now surrounding Bunny. The victim stirred and turned onto his back.

"I'm dead," he confided to Sergeant Weller. "Irrevocably dead! Those two," he said, pointing to Alan and Jane, "were meant to find happiness elsewhere. I shot him and Byron with no effect, no effect whatsoever, can you imagine?"

"Not as well as you, young man," Sergeant Weller said soothingly. "Let's get off the street so you can tell me about it."

"Mommm!" wailed Bunny

On the roof of Alan's car, legs delicately tucked beneath her, Vanessa sat calmly sketching. An audio-visual onslaught had begun. Camera-toting figures snaked their way to stage center while, jumping from car roof to car roof, men with notebooks descended on the stars.

"Oh George, George," wailed Adele, "we've got to get back to the taxi!"

"No!" shouted George proudly "Your almost-ex-husband will hear from you first — in the newspaper tomorrow, on television tonight. You are going to sit before that screen and hold the paper in your hands, and laugh!"

"Oh, George!" she wailed again uncertainly.

★★★★★

"I said quiet," boomed Sergeant Weller, "or I'll lock you up until you're fit to be spoken to."

The authority in her voice and the police station surroundings quelled the verbal riot. The traffic jam was calmly, fairly calmly, explained away: The waiter at Nino's masterfully explained the tragic loss of the rare Crocusiana from Transylvania, snatched by the hand of Alan with the discerning eye. Alan, claiming innocence and love offered additional payment for the flower as well as the return of its somewhat shriveled remains. Adele cited marital distress as the cause of her attendance on the scene, and George echoed a compelling, if not eloquent, "me too." Bunny grumbled something about doing the will of his mother. Had no one seen his mother?

Shouted statements blurred by passion reached their ears from the adjoining room. Sergeant Weller evinced impatience. She had had enough noise for one day. She went next door, six curious human beings close behind her.

"Gilbey!"

"Alan, Jane, you've come! I'm being charged with breaking and entering your apartment."

"Were you?"

"Of course not! You were expecting me."

"Actually, we were hoping you wouldn't come."

"Alan, old school buddy, don't try to get even with me this way. We're friends."

"Friendship is the oldest con game in the world."

"No, Alan, no; not the oldest. Adele, you'll vouch for my character, won't you?"

"I've got myself another lawyer," she said crisply.

"This is unfair."

"I'm sure Adele will get you her lawyer," piped Alan.

Jane gave Alan a strange look. "Do you know this woman?"

"Uh — just her first name. We met briefly."

"In a hotel room," added Gilbey.

"I'm feeling better," offered Bunny.

"Just a moment!" It was Sergeant Weller. "You are not going to air your personal problems in this station house. I have neither the time nor the interest in them. if you can raise bail of fifty dollars you are free to leave until your hearing at ten tomorrow morning. If not ..."

Pockets were emptied.

Alan bent toward Ann Weller. "You're too hard for Byron," he said, in what he thought was a whisper.

"Why should you care? Jane asked, as they headed for the door.

In response, Alan kissed her lightly on the cheek and took her hand in his. "Let's walk, darling. We can pick up the car tomorrow after the hearing."

So they walked, walked through New York at its beautiful spring best.

Jane gave a slight tilt of her head, and they mounted the steps of St. Patrick's Cathedral. Several dozen persons roamed the aisles and sat in the pews.

"Tourists," murmured Alan.

Mounting to the altar from either side Jane saw Saint Francis and St. Jerome. They glowered at each other across the lectern, each waiting for the other to retreat. From between them rose a long-haired woman, thin of face, diaphanous of gown. She took the prayer book in her hands and began to read. Jane strained to hear the words, but heard only shuffling feet and whispered comments, about the carvings, about the art. The vision vanished.

"Hello."

It was Vanessa. Her eyes followed Jane's to the altar. "Did she look out of place to you?"

Involuntarily Janet tightened her hold on Alan's hand.

"Jane, what is — oh, it's you."

Vanessa's laughter rippled through the sanctuary. The tourists shushed her.

"I must remember that. A cherishable greeting. So you don't love me anymore."

"Love you? I never loved you. Jane, she's lying. I swear — !"

"So here you are. I knew if I looked in the most unlikely place I'd find you." It was Bunny.

"Oh no," moaned Alan. "Even in St. Patty's. Why don't you two just go away, disappear. What do you want from us?"

"Nothing anymore, right — uh — Vanessa?"

"That's right, my young marquis, and I hope you've learned your lesson."

Bunny the Marquis sighed. "Yes," he said reluctantly. "I'll behave in the future. Punishment is such a drag. You scared me, though. When I saw these two together, I thought I'd lost my power."

"You'll always be a little boy. There is a power greater than the power of toys. You'll never learn that, I suppose. I knew you would try to play god. 'It's a wise mother who knows her own son,' as the Baron would say."

Bunny laughed. "And you are that mother."

"Quoting the Baron? You?"

"Yes, my dear, me! He sends you love and kisses, no cliché intended."

Jane looked at Vanessa with appreciation. "I'm glad."

"What are you both talking about, and who is the Baron?" demanded Alan.

"A man I met at an art gathering."

"From now on we go to business socials together."

Vanessa smiled approval. "And now I've got a little business to conduct with a certain party."

Alan blanched.

"No, not with you. I think Sergeant Weller would benefit from a little chat with me."

"So I didn't fail completely!" chirped Bunny.

"She'll probably demand the notes you took on the roof of my car."

"Oh, this?" Vanessa produced a pencil sketch from her handbag.

"Hmmm. She looks familiar," said Alan.

Jane's attention was immediately drawn to the paper. "Why, it's Io!"

"You're right," agreed Alan. "It's that Corregio concoction. But there's something wrong with her."

"Everyone wants to be loved," responded Jane defensively.

"Amen to that," said Alan, "but where is the cloud-clothed Jove's embrace? It looks like she's in ecstasy over nothing." He bent low over the sketch. "And are these fingertips or gloves, folds of skin or material? It's not a bad copy for an amateur, is it Jane, but frankly, I can't tell if she's naked or dressed!"

Vanessa smiled faintly. "Does it matter?"

"Well, of course it matters! Our perception of what is happening depends upon it. Is she submitting in mind or in body?"

"Ah, I didn't realize I had to make a choice."

"You're laughing at me." Alan was hurt.

But even as he moped, he suddenly knew this Vanessa he had met in the gallery, among the other art works, this delicate fantasy of flesh and feeling with laughing eyes colored by the quiet daring of a sensuously endless life. She spoke simply, softly, but neither Alan nor Jane failed to hear. "Everyone wants to feel loved."

"My very words to Alan," Jane agreed.

"Not quite," said Vanessa.

"Well — " Alan's mind clutched at the drawing before him. "Well — good luck with Ann Weller, but this sketch will not make a winning introduction to the cruel sergeant. She'll question you even more closely on your devious part in creating the devious traffic jam and the devious cause of your devious disappearance."

"Ah, but you are assuming she was aware of my devious presence. You're right about the sketch, though. Perhaps Jane would like it. The gift of one artist to another."

Jane took the drawing from Vanessa. "I'll keep it always."

Vanessa reclaimed the sketch. "Then you had better live without it. I will not have one of my people cowed by a piece of paper. I must go now."

"You'll be wasting your time talking to Sergeant Weller. She's all business," warned Alan.

"So am I. Say goodbye, Bunny."

"Goodbye. I can't say I'm sorry to be going home, for a while, anyway."

Alan threw up his hands in despair. "Vanessa and her Bunny! I don't completely understand all this Greek!"

Vanessa's infectious laughter tinkled again through the Cathedral. "It's Latin." She brushed a hand on Jane's shoulder. "Happy birthday."

"Jane, good heavens! Your birthday is tomorrow! The opera tickets!"

"Oh, Alan! We've got the hearing in the morning and I've got the Trumbull party tomorrow night. I can't postpone it — the invitations, the preparations! And it's going to be the sensation of the art year. We're supposed to sign a new five-year contract, but I'm dropping him instead. He's the biggest name in the gallery. This will be a headline-maker. Oh, Alan, it will be a new start!"

Alan grinned. "Convinced! The opera is out. Am I out, too?"

"No, darling, you're very much in. I hope your tux still fits you."

"It will fit if I have to hold my breath all night. Let's go home."

At the huge double doors, Alan turned for one last look at the altar.

"You know …" He shook his head.

"Know what, darling?"

"It's silly of course, but I just had a vision of a priest named Father Bema at the lectern."

Jane breathed a sigh, a mingling of enlightenment and peace.

"It's all right, darling. There's room for four."

Jane sniffed the crisp April air with delight. On it floated a timeless song:

"A smile that arrives with the thought of him,
I smile, thinking more than I ought of him,
I don't wax poetic or sing.
The real thing, the real thing.

A laugh that escapes without meaning to,
I laugh at the silly things he can do,
The season I'm feeling is spring.
The real thing, the real thing.

Gone is the dramatic, autocratic mating call,
For love dissolves dramatics and all.

There's warmth that I feel at the sight of him,

Warmth that will light up my life with him,
No foolish daydream or fling.
The real thing, the real thing."

The End